THE PENALTY

A horrifying hockey story.

by Ethan Marek

THE PENALTY

Dedicated to the hockey community

& the state of Minnesota.

Kielstad Knights
vs. Scythes

LEFT WING	CENTER	RIGHT WING

7 — **Finn**
5-8 | 167 | Sophomore
Kielstad, Minn.

5 — **Ben (C)**
5-9 | 174 | Senior
Kielstad, Minn.

12 — **Danny**
5-9 | 187 | Senior
Kielstad, Minn.

21 — **Liam**
5-10 | 185 | Senior
Kielstad, Minn.

3 — **Ash**
5-10 | 182 | Senior
Kielstad, Minn.

19 — **Chester**
5-8 | 166 | Junior
Kielstad, Minn.

LEFT DEFENSE	RIGHT DEFENSE	GOALTENDER

17 — **Jake**
5-11 | 187 | Junior
Kielstad, Minn.

25 — **Charlie**
5-9 | 178 | Junior
Kielstad, Minn.

1 — **Cole**
5-7 | 160 | Senior
Kielstad, Minn.

30 — **Thomas**
5-8 | 180 | Junior
Kielstad, Minn.

HEAD COACH

Coach Kipp

THE SPARK

It's the third period against the Scythes, but yet my blood runs cold. The puck drops on the fresh, mopped ice as the first liners battle their enemies. Ben ties up the centerman as he attempts to kick the puck out with his skate, but of course, no sweat drips from his curly hair. I think my curls are better than his, but it'd look better if it were actually soaked. My hair's so dry and poufy that it wants to push my helmet off, but I should probably stop complaining about it. It's not like Coach Kipp is going to find the comfort to throw me out there, especially when he's the newbie on the team.

Our town of Kielstad couldn't find a suitable person who wanted to run our hockey team, at least not from the school, but instead, they locked us up with an outsider; a division coach. When you work with the division leagues, you better be prepared for the militia's ways of doing; furious competition, accelerating adrenaline, and countless hours of training. But there's one thing coach should know: this is high school, and just because we're playing your old city team doesn't mean you should be scared to play all of your pawns. You barely even know our skills and talents, but you do seem to have a decent understanding of our last year's stats.

Their centerman throws the puck back to his left defenseman from the faceoff. Danny, our right winger, does his job on the right side of the ice and pushes towards the Scythes' defenseman, but the defenseman passes the puck to his other defenseman. Finn, left winger, skates inside-out from the center dot and pushes the other defenseman towards the Scythes' bench. He skates and skates towards the guy, about to flip him upside down and into his own bench, at least that's what everybody thinks is going to happen. I know how it works though. Finn can never lay down a hit on a player. He's always too busy trying to dangle with the fricken puck, and he's too scared to bash the bigger guys down! I swear, it feels like the game can be in the grasp of my hands, but if only Coach Kipp would play our line.

The puck is thrown into our defensive zone. This is the beginning of turnovers central. The first liners can never break the puck out of the zone, and it's so embarrassing! Even during a power play, if we're lucky, they can't find a way to break that frickin black disk out of our zone without icing the damn thing, and you wonder why we're losing this game 0-4. Coach gets pissed at the first liners to where his face burns its own wildfire, but he never budges the thought to take the first liners off the ice because they're "extraordinary." Okay, coach, I understand that

2

they have a lot of points, but do you even realize why my line barely has points? We never get played! Oh my God! I am the most hardworking individual on this team! I don't understand why Ben is the fucking captain. I don't understand why my line is never the first line of a game. I don't understand why coach never plays us in these fricken games, no matter how much first line sucks!

While I stand on this bench in my own thoughts, the rain clouds build inside of me, ready to downpour all the way home. Our student section chants our team on to our no-hope victory and the hockey parents watch the game in their little gossip groups. My mom sits all alone, and I can see her staring at me from the middle of the bleachers. I know what she's thinking. I'm thinking the exact same thing, but her perspective is totally different from mine.

My mother is one of those moms who wants me to succeed in life, which is great! What mother wouldn't want their child to be successful? But she wants me to succeed in hockey so she can prove to the other moms that their kids aren't exactly stellar athletes who are bound for the college leagues. That's how small-town hockey works. If your kid's an elite hockey player, or any elite player for a sport's team, then the parents think they're all celebrities. Even the coaches invite them for a drink at a local restaurant of some sort. The parents hangout with the coaches and the coaches make the parents like them by playing their kids in the games. After this hockey game, the first game of the season, I'm going straight to my room to cry my eyes out till they dry into sand dunes.

An alarming whistle brings my attention back to the game. What a shocker. The referee raises his right arm straight in the air, looking right at Finn who lies flat on the ice. Finn hops onto his feet as the ref takes his arm and drops it forward. He took a tripping penalty, the weakest penalty of them all. If you're stupid enough to take a tripping penalty because you're that slow and weak, then maybe coach should think again about putting me out there.

"Liam, Ash," coach says. Me and Ash look back at coach, but then we meet bulging eyes. "Go. They need a breather." Oh. That makes more sense. First liners need a breather. "Forty-five seconds and I want you guys off." We head out onto the ice.

Should I get off the ice in forty-five seconds? No way! This is my chance to shine! What if I were to block the Scythes' defenseman from sniping a shot by our blue line? What if the puck bolted right into my shin pad? The crowd would react in pain with their hands covering their mouths, thinking that it hurt or something, but I wouldn't feel a thing! The puck would bounce off my pad and it'd hop behind the defenseman. I'd shred the ice with my speed like a cheese grater grating swiss cheese, and I'd take the puck on a short-handed breakaway. I'd curl my stick's blade forward so it's almost parallel with the ice, pull my stick back to my waist's height, and then, I'd make contact with the puck. My stick would bend into taffy, and then I'd slingshot the puck to the top right corner of the goalie's net. The puck would then frisbee in the air as the goalie lifts his catcher's glove up, but he'd react too fast. The puck would fly right under his glove and hit the netting for a goal on the scoreboard. The students would jump and scream in complete joy, holding a sign with my name and number on it: Liam #21. My teammates would slam their sticks on the boards as coach would try to keep his serious composure. But that's only the facade of it all. I know Ben would be pissed with saltiness inside his thin skull, and coach would think highly of himself; he'd be the reason for our team scoring a goal. But to be honest, we don't have a true team. Our team is fighting two battles at the same time: one is the game itself, and the other is the mystical tension between the first liners and my line, but we can't seem to talk it out.

Me and Ash skate up to the left circle in our defensive zone. He moves to his center position on the dot and I go to my right side hashmarks. I get into a weird angle stance, like when you're supposed to write in a notebook with the book actually crooked so you can write neater. I bend my right leg, and once that puck drops, I'm pushing off the ice with my left and charging for it.

The referee blows his whistle, clarifying that the two-minute penalty is up and ready on the scoreboard, and skates to the dot. The puck drops and I bolt behind the Scythe's centerman. Ash battles for the puck as it slides towards Jake and Charlie, our only defensemen on the team. Jake picks up the puck and goes behind Cole's net.

Cole is our main goalie for the team. We have a backup goalie, Thomas, and I swear he's in the same boat as me. Thomas rarely gets played, Cole is always going to be coach's pick, and

I've wanted to talk to him about it, but he's always having a blast and cheering the team on. I'm pretty sure he can care less about playing or not. As long as he is a part of the team, he's living a great life. I don't know how he lives with it.

Jake wraps the puck around the net and slaps it off the high glass for icing. The puck slides all the way to the other end. The goalie rolls out of his net and sets the puck up for his defenseman. As they skate up, I know I'm supposed to do what coach has told us to do in a situation like this. I need to cut inside-out, skate through the middle of the ice and target the player with the puck on the outside while deflecting any kind of pass they can make. So, I skate through the middle and time out their defenseman. He builds up speed and skates the puck towards his bench. I turn left and target for a clean hit to knock the puck off his stick, but he manages to pass the puck through my stick and over to the other defenseman. Ash rushes over to him, then the defenseman pushes the puck into our zone. The defenseman rolls down to the bottom corner of Cole's net, but no one approaches the puck. We're supposed to have someone approach the player with the puck!

"Charlie! That's you!" Jake yells.

As a defenseman, Charlie's the one needing to attack the low guy. The player skates towards the net as Charlie begins to skate at him, but it's too late. The Scythes' defenseman shoots a tricky angle shot, right on the back of Cole's leg, and it bounces right in. The guy slides on both his knees to his student crowd as I hop back onto the bench with Ash. Coach Kipp clenches his jaw, crumples the lineup in his fist, and watches the Scythes' crowd

6

cheer their team on to victory. Finn exits the penalty box with his head hanging down, skating over to the bench.

"Finn!" coach says. "Stay out there and finish this God damn game with your line!"

Great. This game is pure torture. There's a weird sense of guilt that builds inside of me, but I couldn't have done anything about that goal. That wasn't my job to stop that defenseman. Sure, I could've blocked the pass, but that was outside of our zone, not the biggest deal in the world. We should be capable of putting on a fight during a penalty kill in our own zone! We could have more goals if coach played us, but no, the first liners are so much better than us.

The buzzer blares its horn. The game is over, a tremendous 5-0 lost against the Scythes. My line, and Thomas, hop off the bench as the first liners beat us to Cole, patting him on the head and saying *good game*, but what about that game was good? So, I skate to Cole and say, "Good job." I didn't want to make it seem like I was a jerk and say, "Put in more effort next time," but I didn't want to lie to him and say *good game*. At least I hope he understands that the game was fucking awful. It's not his fault for the loss of the game, but he is friends with the first liners, and he could be telling them to put in more work like I do. Every day, after school, we get an hour-and-a-half before practice starts. I usually go to team yoga, but the first liners always skip. Ben thinks it's pointless and not a good use of their time. They'd rather go to the sub shop and buy sub sandwiches, adding more calories to the fat they already have.

Whatever Ben says, Danny and Cole always agree with him because he's gold in their eyes. He's popular! Everybody loves Ben, even the teachers get caught up in his stupid life. It's so annoying how much that kid becomes the teacher's pet. He's always commented by them about how smart and talented he is, and they don't even care what he does in class. His grades are straight A's and he's just a stellar athlete for the school. Ben also plays football. He isn't the best at it, but when you're on the football team and play on a decent line, you're automatically popular in high school.

It's really weird why Finn follows Ben and his posse around school though. Finn is just so introverted, but I guess he gets the benefits Ben receives. Maybe I should just be friends with Ben and I'd finally play during a game! No way. He doesn't want to catch my disease of the benchwarmer.

After we shake hands with the other team, we walk off the ice and back into the locker room. I take a seat on the bench over by the back wall, next to my best friends, Chester and Ash. Me and Ash have played together since middle school while our dads coached the team. It's kind of funny how we're friends because we seem to be total opposites; Ash is totally extroverted while I'm a settled introvert. Chester seems to be a mix of an extrovert and introvert. He's either hanging out with friends or working on his own activities. The three of us have gotten a nickname over the years. Our parents like to call us The Beasts. We're apparently really terrifying and ferocious out on the ice, but of course, our new coach probably doesn't see that.

Thomas enters, then he sits on our left at the end of the bench, and the rest of the guys sit in front of us, closer to the door. Once Cole walks in, the door seals shut, and the silence floods the locker room. We all sit in the quiet, waiting for coach to walk in and give us a vicious pep talk.

The cumulonimbus clouds thicken inside my head, ready to pour out what's been floating inside throughout the game. What a great fucking start to the season. I really hope this isn't how my last year of high school is gonna go. How am I a senior in high school and not receiving any playing time? Finn's a fricken sophomore, and he gets way more playing time than me! I just want to be on the school bus and call it done for the night.

The locker room door opens. Coach's head peers around the corner. "Finn," he says. "Come here."

Finn takes his helmet off and throws it down into his hockey bag. He stands and walks out of the locker room, his skate blades clicking along the way. Screw it, I'm going to take my gear off and get out of this locker room. Once I take my helmet and jersey off, Ash and Chester decide to do the same. I look over to Ben, and I can see him looking me down, probably wondering why I'm taking my gear off, but I don't care at this point. This room topples upon me with its thick walls of depression. Maybe the concrete ceiling can randomly topple on top of me and crack my skull open.

Let the blood flow its own river, it can find its way out.

THE BARN

The kids from the student section wait in the lobby, looking for the few individuals. My mother probably left the arena already, it's getting quite late, and I'm sure none of the parents wanted to talk to her with the amount of playing time I got. While I walk through the lobby and towards the front doors, some of the kids from my school watch me pass. I can see a few whispers wiggle out from their mouths. The parents block my way to the door. I push my way through by squeezing through the small gaps. Some of the parents make eye contact with me, but they don't say a word, not even a smile grows upon their face. Once I pass through the crowd, I make my way through the front doors. And just like last year, no one cares about me. No one cares to say anything to me after the game, and I have no friends from the student section to talk to.

Our school bus waits along the sidewalk as the cool breeze swifts the industrial fuel into the night's air. I walk inside of the back trailer. I set my hockey bag down on the right side of the trailer, and I realize I left the locker room in such a hurry that I forgot to put my hockey stick in the stick bag. Oh well. I'll just lay it under my bag.

Once I exit the trailer, I walk along the bus towards its double doors. All the windows cover in fog as the bus is our team's sauna. The bus rides are awesome during the night because it's the time when I can just sit back and relax in the warm, cozy heat. But this bus ride is going to be different. I'm ready to release all of my pain that has been trapped inside of me. My chest feels like it's suffocating on the inside with all the feelings I have right now.

I find a seat in the middle of the bus and sit down, hanging my jersey on the window and blocking the view of the parking lot. I want to cry right now, but the lights are on, and people will see me with my head down. Fine, I'll just wait till the whole team gets on, and once those lights are off, I'll let my silent Hell flood a lake beneath my feet.

After a while of sitting alone on the bus, I can feel a set of feet walking up the front steps. I look towards the front to find Chester entering the bus. What do I do? Do I keep my head down or do I look at my phone? Do I look at him and say good job? No, that last one is completely stupid! We didn't even play in the game! Oh my, he's coming closer. Just act like you're doing something with your fingernails.

Suddenly, my phone slips from my pocket and bangs onto the floor and into the middle of the aisle, right in front of Chester. He stops and picks up my phone, handing it to me.

11

"Thanks, Chester," says I.

"Anything for my friend," he says.

Chester smiles, but I can't seem to discover where my smile is at the moment. It's probably hiding in its grave, ready to be buried alive for life. He ends up sitting directly behind me, but I wonder if he feels down at all. He does like cross country better than hockey, but I'm going to have to talk to him about it sometime, and Ash. This is just unbelievable, and where are the other slackers? Come on! Every single second, my heart sinks deeper into my stomach. I can't hold in the pain anymore.

I look across the aisle to the right side of the bus and out the window. Silhouettes carrying hockey bags out of the arena finally walk outside to the back of the bus. The boys start loading the bus, and it's always the same seating arrangement with the first liners sitting in the back seats and the others sitting near me in the middle seats. I don't even want to see Ben's face right now. So, I'm just going to look down into the darkness and feel the heat from the heaters blow upon my face. I can hear the squeaky footsteps walk down the aisle, and I feel every shadow that passes my body, bodies that obstruct the dim bus lights.

Hopefully, the bus can leave coach behind at the rink, or maybe coach can ride with someone else back home. I just don't want to see him or else he might see a catastrophic outbreak from me. Slowly, I peer to the front of the bus as someone else is boarding. It's Finn, but not the same Finn I saw before.

Finn holds a bloody paper towel up to his nose with his face containing dry blood on his cheeks and a long scratch that stretches his whole forehead. He has two black eyes; one is more purple than the other. He finds a seat out front on the other side and sits down. Finn never sits in the front of the bus. He always sits in the back with Ben's group. Geezes, did I miss something during the hockey game? Oh! Maybe it happened during that one penalty . . . No. There's no way because he was the one who tripped the Scythes' player, and he never got into a fight.

As I watch Finn hide in the bus seat, coach enters the bus and sits down in his reserved seat, way up in the first seat on the bus. Every day, coach thinks he's VIP, always needing things done his way. I think he has anger issues because if we screwed up a drill in practice with minor mishaps, he would turn into a black crow and fly widely all over the ice, whipping his stick against the boards and spitting in front of all our faces, getting his message across about perfection. He always says in practice, "If you guys can't do a simple drill, then how do you expect to win a fucking hockey game."

The lights on the bus shut off as the front doors seal us all in the sauna. The bus jolts a tear out of my eye as it moves forward. I can't hold it in any longer, and I silently sob in the tight corner of my bus seat. I pull my sweatshirt hood over my beanie hat and tuck my face towards my jersey which hangs from the window. The tears are never going to stop on this bus ride, but I'll have to stop about five minutes before home so my eyes can dry out. Usually, I would put my headphones on, but I'm too depressed to even listen to music. My nose begins to clog with snot as I try to flush out my system.

After about ten minutes, my tank doesn't even feel like it's halfway empty. I keep crying through the dark countryside. I grab the bottom of my jersey and lift it up, peeking outside into the nothingness. Everything appears black; the moon is probably covered up by the cloudy skies, but maybe there's a new moon, which would make sense with the dark emotions I have.

Suddenly, I feel a thud next to me on my seat. I glance over to find Finn, staring at me with his frozen tears. He can definitely see my river of tears flowing down my cheeks. I didn't stop crying but seeing his beat-up face made my first instinct to hug him. We silently hug while our tears drip down each other's back.

"Finn," says I. "What happened?"

I grab Finns' shoulders and push them away from me, only so I can look him in the eyes and hear the truth from him. He just stares at me, developing more tears to stream down his face into his soft lips.

"Finn, talk to me, bud," says I.

Finn wipes his eyes with his sweatshirt sleeve and sniffles back some snot.

"I don't know what I did wrong," he says.

"Finn, what did he say to you?"

"He said I embarrassed him."

Finn wants to downpour more rain, but I need to keep him together. "How did you embarrass him?" says I. "What did he say?"

"He said my penalty brought great disgrace to the team."

I push his hair back to look at the big scratches carved into his forehead.

"Did he do this to you?" says I.

Finn shakes his head no, looking down at the ground and wiping his nose with his sleeve.

"Did he do this to you?" says I, more firmly to him this time.

"He said if I told anyone, he wouldn't play me anymore," he says.

Finn breaks out and leans against me. I hug him tightly to my body as his head rests upon my flat shoulder. My sweatshirt soaks up in tears and I start to look like I put some work in today, but it doesn't matter at this point. No one is going to see any of it now. I just wish I could have played some hockey! I love this fucking sport, and I would do anything to play it all day long! Me and Finn cry out the rest of the bus ride in the soft, snowy winter night.

The bus bumps over some railroad tracks, and it's a good sign that we made it back to The Barn, our hockey arena. We call it The Barn because it was refurbished from an old farm shed and had the perfect size to fit a sheet of ice. Our high school team has a locker room which holds nine-foot wooden stalls for our gear. We all sit together and put on our gear before practice and games in that locker room. That's the only time I ever feel like we're somewhat close together as a team, but the first liners decide to sit in the front near the white board, acting like these huge leaders on the team.

We pull up to the front set of doors to The Barn, and we all get up in a hurry, ready to leave the steamy sauna. Coach leaves first and heads inside of the arena. I head outside towards the back of the bus with Finn, and we open up the trailer door. Other hockey bags are piled on top of mine. The first liners barge into the trailer and grab their bags in a hurry. Cole throws one of the bags in the snow so he can take out his goalie pads and hockey bag. Finn searches the trailer for his bag as I can finally see mine, sitting at the bottom of the trailer with my hockey stick. I'm the last one to grab my hockey bag, and Finn is confused as to where his bag went.

"Finn, is this your bag?" says I.

I point to the bag that Cole threw in the snow, and it's for sure his bag. After closing the trailer, Finn and I walk into the arena together as the school bus leaves the empty parking lot.

The arena is dark and quiet since it's roughly midnight. We pass through the concession area and walk to the long, endless hallway. The ceiling rafters are so high up and the hallway seems to be an eighth of a mile long. We walk down the crucially long hallway, passing the window and door of the dryland room. The next door on the left, which is still a long walk down, is our locker room. A smaller hallway later forks off to the left which contains coach's locker room, and then another door even further down the hallway includes the girls' locker room. A set of french doors at the end of the hallway on the right is our entrance to the ice. These are the game doors. This is where our team skates out for practices and games. The dog pound cheers us on from the bleachers as we run out onto the fresh sheet of ice.

Finn and I walk into the locker room. I set my hockey stick in the stick stand and walk around to where our stalls are located.

The first two stalls on the left belong to Ben and Danny. They're putting their gear away in a rush. On the right, Finn's stall is the first one, then it's Ash's, mine, and Thomas' stall. Charlie and Jake sit along the back wall with Cole, that's where the defensemen usually sit.

I hustle to get all my gear out of my bag to drought itself in more humid air. I start by hanging my jersey on the back hook and my bulky breezers on the left hook. Next, I hang my chest pads on the right hook. My helmet and gloves go way up to the tippy top of the stall, and my elbow pads and knee pads slide into a small shelf under my helmet. I hang my skates on two plastic holders at the top of the stall as the laces dangle off. Water will periodically drip from the skates and into my hair, but tonight, they're completely dry. Now, I can throw my bag with everything else in the bottom cubby holder. I grab my car keys and my phone, ready to leave the locker room.

When I turn around, I notice some of the other guys had left the locker room already. Ben, Danny, and Cole have all left, and Ash is just heading out the door. As I make my way to the door, I give Finn a pat on the back. He doesn't even turn around to look. He starts to put his gear away in his stall as I head out of the locker room.

DEPTHS OF DARKNESS

Finn and Thomas are the last guys in the locker room. Thomas is busy screwing his mask onto his goalie helmet. Finn sits and stares at the wall like he's looking out from the inside of his own painting. He's motionless, quiet, and it catches Thomas' attention. Thomas finishes screwing his mask in and stands up, setting his helmet on the top of his stall. He walks towards the front door but stops in front of Finn, raising his chin up with his hand. Finn looks at him in the eyes.

"You alright, Finn?" Thomas says.

"Yeah, I'm fine," he says.

"Come along. We're the last ones here."

Finn looks back at the stalls in front of him.

"I'll be out soon," Finn says. "I just need a few minutes alone."

Thomas seems to hesitate to say something for a second, but he walks away and leaves the locker room. Finn sits in the silence, alone, staring at Ben's stall in front of him. Finn walks over to the locker room's bathroom where a mirror hangs over the sink. He looks into the mirror at his beat-up face. He takes his hand and caresses it against a huge black mark on the side of his face. He turns the sink on and pours water into his hand. His head ducks down by the sink as he tries to wipe off the black mark on his cheek. Once he gets it off, he looks back into the mirror and looks straight into his bruised, black eyes.

Finn leaves the locker room and walks down the long hallway towards the front of the arena. He wipes his tears away with his sweatshirt sleeve and passes the dryland room, but as he walks along, the door of the dryland room opens. Ben appears from the darkness. He grabs Finn's body from behind, wrapping his arms around his waist. Finn yells in fear.

Ben pulls him into the dryland room, then the light from the hallway shines on Danny's face as he shuts the dryland room's door.

"We should take him outside so there's no blood on the floor," Danny says.

"What are you doing to me?" Finn cries out.

Ben holds onto Finn as they leave the dryland room through another door that leads to the outdoor rink. Danny walks out of the dryland room, and Cole fades out from the darkness too. Cole shuts the door behind him, and they trudge through the ankle-deep snow to the outdoor ice.

The rough ice is lit by two towering light poles and surrounds with pine trees. No homes are nearby, just the darkness of a pine needle forest and The Barn. Danny runs in front of Ben and opens the metal gate to the outdoor ice. Ben walks Finn onto the ice who struggles to escape from his hold. Once they reach the center of the ice, Ben keeps hold to Finn's body as Danny takes Finn's sweatshirt hood and flips it over his head, tightening and tying it on his face. Ben whips his body down onto the ice and all three of them walk over to him. Finn tries to get up, but Ben throws a hard kick into his gut. Finn chokes on his own cough and tries to call for help, but nothing comes out. Ben throws another kick at his gut as Danny comes around and kicks him in the back. Cole stands back and watches it all in delight.

"You fucking fool," Ben says.

Ben throws another kick into his gut. Danny keeps repeatedly kicking Finn in the back. Ben gets down on top of Finn and puts him on his back. Danny stops kicking.

"You embarrassed us," Ben says. He rips open Finn's hood and rips a punch to the side of Finn's head. "You embarrassed all of us!" Ben whips another punch to Finn's head, his nose and mouth bleeding out a blood stream. "Coach is pissed at us now, thanks to you!"

Ben lifts up Finn's head and releases his final words as he throws his head into the surface of the ice, "Fuck . . . YOU!"

A blood puddle covers the ice under Finn's head. Ben, Danny, and Cole walk off the ice. Finn lays onto his side to let the blood drip from his mouth. His head bangs in pain with it feeling heavy and thick. The outdoor lights shut off as Finn lays on the ice in the dark. He stares at the clouds from above where the moon peeks through the ominous clouds. The white light shimmers the blood tears that fill Finns' eyes. He begins to crawl his way to the gate. He's able to stand up and limps his way out. A trail of blood is left behind to stain the ice.

Finn hops into his car and drives to his home which sits on Cedar Lake. His house appears to be a bigger version of the in-town suburban homes. The driveway lights shine up the snow-covered driveway as he pulls the car in front of the left stall. Finn opens up his car door and slowly exits. He shuts the door and walks into the snowbank on the side of the house. Finn crisscrosses his arms and holds himself tightly, shivering in the midst of the cool moonlit night. He trudges his feet through the sticky snow as he approaches the backyard which is lit by the deck lights. He walks down a huge hill, starting from his house and ending at the lakeside. The light illuminates Finn's face, and it looks as if he turned into a cannibal and has eaten a sickening meal of raw, bloody meat.

Finn's mother leaves the front door of the house and walks out to the front doorsteps in her slippers and robe. She peeks into the driveway and calls out for Finn, but no response. She walks out into the snow and finds his car. She walks over to the car but notices a blood trail leading from the driver side door and into the snowbank, followed by footprints.

Finn reaches the shoreline. A hockey net sits in the snow beside the frozen lake. He grabs it from the snow and sets it on the ice. He grasps the metal crossbar from behind him and pulls the net out onto the surface of the lake. His mother's voice echoes from the house.

"Finn?" she says.

Finn ignores his mother and keeps on walking out to the middle of the dark, frozen lake. His mother trudges faster and faster through the snow towards him.

"Finn! It's not safe out there!"

Finn keeps on walking and she begins to lose sight of him.

"FINN, STOP!"

Finn stops. He stands in place as his mother trudges to the shoreline. She freezes.

"Finn! What's wrong!?"

Finn turns around and looks at his mother. Her jaw drops, and she covers her mouth with her hand. She notices all the beatings on his face. His nose is crooked, his eyes appear to be blackholes sucking in the darkness, and his jaw is completely covered in dry blood. He grasps his frozen, pale hands onto the crossbar of the net and looks into his mother's eyes.

"I love you, mom!"

"FINN! NO!"

Finn grabs the net as he forces himself to fall backwards into an unfrozen hole in the lake. He crashes through the thin coating of ice as the hockey net topples on top of him. His body is pulled down by the inside netting of the hockey net. His mother screams the clouds away as the moon shines down onto the hole. She runs out to it and sees Finn's body sinking into the abyss. Finn looks his mother dead in the eyes for the last time before he disappears into the depths of darkness.

NIGHT CHILLS

It takes a breath in the night for me to recognize that I had just awoken from something terrifying. Too much happened at once during the devil's hour. There's no way I can close my eyes again and attempt to doze off, just to find myself awakening in another paralyzed state. The only thing that lights up my bedroom is the moonlight that shines its blasting cold white through my frosted window. My room must've lost heat because my breath fogs up right in front of my eyes. Well, if I'm not going to fall asleep, then I might as well go fix myself a snack.

I hop out from my furry blankets and slide on my nighttime slippers. I walk over to the door and twist the doorknob as quiet as I can to avoid disturbance with my mother, right next door to my bedroom. Now, I have to walk pass her door on the creaky wooden pine floors and down the steps without slipping. As I tiptoe against the creaky floors and pass my mother's door, I can now walk down the steps and go inside the kitchen.

Our house has a basic log cabin feel to it. The home heats by a wood furnace which might explain why it's so cold inside. Mother must've not cared too much about warming up the place. I can warm up with the fireplace in the living room, but then I would have to wait for the wood to burn to its dusty ashes. Maybe hot chocolate would do for the night. Yes! That's a great idea, but I also need to add marshmallows. Not those big marshmallows, only the mini marshmallows that you find in Swiss Mix! Those are the sugar bombs!

I walk into the kitchen and grab my hockey mug. The colors on the hockey mug are based off of my team's colors: maroon, black, and white. Our school's color was originally a cardinal red, but over the years, the color adapted to maroon. Good thing the color changed or else we'd look just like the Scythes.

Great. Trying to keep my mind off of things, Liam.

I open up our stainless-steel refrigerator, which is cold to the touch, and pull out the gallon of one-percent milk. When I pour the milk into the mug, it hits the bottom and flows into the air like a floating river defying gravity. The milk fills up to approximately three quarters, and that means it's time to microwave the milk for two minutes. I set the hockey mug in the microwave and quickly type in two minutes as the beeps alarm inside of my mind. As the microwave counts down, I walk into the dining room and sit upon a pine chair.

I don't know if I'll be able to fall asleep. Why is that nightmare sending chills down my spine? It's like the chills were going through my veins and frosting up my fingertips and toes. I was sitting beside my mother in the car, she was driving the SUV in the middle of a snowy night. The headlights would shine but they couldn't make it through the cosmic fluff, blowing in the typhoon winds. We were driving on a smooth path, but there was no road in sight. There's only the snow that coats the surface of this soft, mattress ground. My mother pulled the car into the driveway of our home. As we pulled up to the driveway, the headlights shone through the falling white ashes. The garage door was opened, and my father appeared to be sleeping while standing by his work shelf. His back was towards us, but I could see about half of his face lying upon the shelf. Honk! My heart sunk into my gut as my mother honked at my father in the crepuscular garage. I looked at my father as one of his eyes darted open, and he stared at me with the satanic eye of the devil. The darkness begun to cave in around the car and melted my pale flesh to the bone. I was in shock, and I didn't know what to do. Mother fidgeted with her seat belt and buckled it up. I looked back to my father who closed his eye and lifted his head off the shelf. His face twisted a hundred and eighty degrees towards me as his body rotated with it. His other eye flashed open. My mother put the car in reverse and pressed the pedal to the floor. The car jumped backwards for a second but halted as my mother's seat broke. Her body flew back to the car's floor as she struggled to get back up. I looked over to my father again. He was walking towards me like a zombie, ready to stare his soul into my throbbing eyes of terror. I ducked down under the airbag dash and watched my passenger side window. He walked up to the window and turned his body towards the door.

He turned his head to find me sitting on the floor in panic.

Beep!

I come back to reality finding my milk has warmed. I take the mini-marshmallow-hot-chocolate-mix packet, tear its thin white packaging open, and dump it into the scorching milk. I grab a teaspoon and stir the mix into the milk to get all the chocolate dissolved. The mug burns my hand, and I always think to myself, what if this hot mug just broke in my hand? How painful would it be to have shards of hot glass in the palm of my hand? Honestly, nothing can defeat the pain that I felt from last night's game.

I take my hockey mug by the warm handle and carry it over to the dining table. When I drink my hot chocolate, I always love to alternate the usage of my teaspoon and just straight up drinking the hot chocolate from the mug. I fish for the mini marshmallows with my tiny teaspoon, and it's the most satisfying feeling in the world. But you can't just eat all the marshmallows immediately! That's why I alternate because if there aren't any mini marshmallows in the drink, then I'm not as motivated to finish the drink.

A cool breeze strikes my left shoulder and my lower leg. It's the same feeling when it's fall and you get a nice, relaxing breeze that makes you feel like you're at an awkward point in your life. Fall always feels awkward to me. The trees and leaves rot and die in the drizzling rain, and the temperature buries itself into the cold dirt ground, but this breeze is much colder since it's winter. The window is open, inviting the bitter air into our house. The drapes wave ghostly hellos to me as I get nearer and nearer to the window. An owl whoos from the forest surrounding our home. I feel like I'm being stalked by this owl, but I close the window and untie the drapes to blanket it from the outside.

I chug down my luscious hot chocolate and tiptoe back up the pine wood stairs to my bedroom. Whenever I shut my bedroom door, I always peer into the darkness of the hallway. There's always some sort of sense that something is down there in the never-ending space. I flush my door shut and lock it up to seal myself in my room.

I hop into bed and find a picture of my dad and me hanging on the wall. That was the first day of bantams in my eighth-grade year. My father has coached me and the team every single year of our lives. He'd always set up the coolest tournaments to where we could miss school on Friday, and then we'd travel up north in our frigid state of Minnesota. He also made our late-night practices a blast with all the scrimmages and games we got to compete our teammates in. Since my dad was the head coach, I always got the advantage to play first line, but he was a great coach because he always switched the lines around. That's the best thing a hockey team could do because there's nothing better than learning how to work with all of your teammates. When a team of boys work together and have fun together, that's when the true chemistry kicks in to play. I'm so proud of my father! When it came to my first high school hockey game, sophomore year, my father was on his way to making the away game in Chaska. As he was driving along some icy country roads, out on County Road 21, he slipped on black ice and his foot must have never came off of the pedal.

His car drifted into a parked combine right outside of a crop field. I never understood why there was a combine in the field during the winter, but the cops discovered something else about the accident. The black ice wasn't the big icebreaker. Snow fluffed up inside of the exhaust pipe and froze over, blocking all the carbon monoxide emissions from escaping the vehicle. My father slowly suffocated, and he didn't even realize it, and he never got to watch me play in a high school hockey game.

SUPERNOVA

A knocking rampage at my bedroom door wakes me up in the morning sun. The light shines upon my window, brightening up the darkness that lurked around last night. The new day is the resurrection with the sunlight beaming its comfortable warmth back into my room. The constant bangs on my door are followed with my name.

"Liam," one voice says.

"Liam," another voice says. "Open up!"

I throw my stiff legs off the bed and walk over to the door, accidently stubbing my toe against my nightstand. I unlock the door and open it to find Chester and Ash stuck in mud.

"You guys gonna come in or what," says I.

Chester and Ash unfreeze themselves and walk into my room. I shut the door behind them to keep my mother out of the conversation; who knows what they want to talk about.

"What time is it," says I.

"Almost ten," Chester says.

I'm sorta shocked when he said it was only ten o'clock in the morning. It feels a lot more like noon with the sun straight up in the sky. The sunlight hours in the winter are crucially short, lasting from eight in the morning to five in the afternoon. After that, the darkness just spills back into the sky.

"Liam," Ash says. "We have something to tell you."

"What? What is it?"

Chester and Ash look at each other in a brief pause. They can't just leave me hanging like an icicle, melting in the beaming sunrise.

"There's no easy way to put this," Chester says.

"Finn committed suicide last night," Ash says.

The world stops spinning at this very moment. The sun freezes and the trees bend their tops towards me. The birds stop and stare through the unfrosted windows, and the air thins itself to the point of drifting off into the vast blackness of space. I wanted to cry a storm, but the tears hibernate inside of me. I can't discover my feelings about this. I look up at Ash and Chester, but they don't have any signs of tears. Maybe they cried it out earlier.

"Liam," Ash says.

I look at them both in the eyes and wrap my arms around them. We hug till the world turns on again with the sun striking down upon us.

The next thing I know, the three of us pull up into Finn's driveway to find police cars and an ambulance parked out front in the frozen snow. The temperature is at an outstanding negative one-degree fahrenheit today, slowing down my train of thought. Ash parks the car behind a police car, then we go towards the side of his house. Walking down the side of the house, I can see a messy blood trail in the snow that leads my eye all the way down to the lake. A group of officers and an FBI agent stand around the hole in the lake with Finn's mother and father, hugging each other with a furry blanket wrapped around them.

We hustle through the snow and make it to the frozen lake. It's a long run out to the middle of the lake, but the lake is a glorious masterpiece in a skater's peace of mind. We reach the hole of the lake as Ash, Chester, and I give Finn's parents a comforting hug. Bubbles float up to the top of the ice water as a scuba diver pops out with Finn's frostbitten body. His mother drops to her knees as she screams the pain away, cracking the ice across the whole lake.

Finn's body is indescribable. The water is frozen around his body, and his skin is whiter than a flash explosion of a star. It's too hard for any of us to look at him without our hearts sinking into the depths of the frozen lake. This day just feels like any other awkward Sunday but add the awful event of losing a fellow teammate. The one day of healing turned into a one-day blizzard; I can't seem to see anything through this violent Hell.

Later that day, Finn's parents and our team bury him under center ice inside of The Barn for remembrance. We will always remember Finn as a shy, quiet, but a remarkable, innocent human being. His coffin slowly drops through the concrete ground and into the frozen soil below. As the mother and father watch their child bellow into the cold ground, I can see Ben staring the mother down with bulging eyes. I look back to the coffin as I watch Finn's parents throw toys of his into their son's pit. All the parents who come and support our games watch the sobering event too, but my mother couldn't make it. She works in the cities as a nurse, and no one gets a break in the healthcare industry. Once the funeral finishes, the arena manager floods the section with water and freezes it over.

I glance back over to Ben to find him making his way over to me. He just stares at me the entire time with some devious look inside. He approaches me and puts his dry mouth to my ear.

"Coach wants to talk," he says.

THE PIZZERIA

I find myself sitting in my locker room stall, surrounded by my
teammates with the worst feeling of guilt floating around the
room. I'm confused why Finn would do something so
traumatizing. The only explanation that would make sense is how
Coach Kipp beat the hell out of him that night, but there has to be
more than that! Finn's tough! He wouldn't just give up on life
because of a few painful bruises, he's stronger than that! Speaking
of coach, he walks through the locker room door and paces
through the middle of our stalls. I look around at the other guys to
find them all staring something down. Chester stares at the floor,
Ben looks across to Finn's stall, Thomas plays with his fingernails,
Cole looks at a soccer ball on the floor, and Jake and Charlie
watch coach pace up and down the aisle. Suddenly, coach stops
pacing by the stick stand. It's amazing how instant the tension
bends the room.

    Coach Kipp turns around and kicks the stick stand. It slams

onto the ground as the hockey sticks bang and bounce off the floor, blocking the exit to the endless hallway.

"How do you feel?" he yells. "How do you all feel that one of your teammates is dead?" No one answers. His anger builds with every strong moment of silence. "He killed himself because he didn't feel loved. He killed himself because he didn't have any support from his fucking team!" The tension that fluxes in the air pushes down my throat. "I'm going to leave you guys, all of you guys, with one question. Why are you guys playing hockey, and what did you get from all of this?"

The tension drifts away into the air vents as the atmosphere settles on top of our heads. Coach walks over to the stick stand and lifts it back up to its rectangular wooden base. He throws and kicks all the hockey sticks away from the door. He leaves the room while we're all trapped inside of our thoughts.

I'm too nervous to even look any of my teammates in the eyes. Everyone is so depressed. An overcast cloud casts above us, creating an awkward dreary environment in this very room. All I'm doing is shaking off my anxiety with my leg and trying to recoup everything that has happened within the last twenty-four hours. I can feel the immense pounding of a migraine building up inside my brain. A drink of water and some food might help cope with the headache, but no one's making a move. No one's getting up to leave the locker room. Everyone's still like the naked trees, and quiet like the dead of a winter night.

Finally, after a long while of sitting in a dead forest, Ben, Danny, and Cole leave together. Eventually, Jake and Charlie follow out from behind them. Chester, Ash, Thomas, and I are the only ones left in the locker room. My stomach rumbles, and that's my signal to talk to them.

"Hey," says I. "Do you guys wanna get something at Carbone's?"

We all end up hopping into my car and riding over to Carbone's Pizzeria. A huge pepperoni pizza sounds tremendous right now. I don't remember the last time I'd eaten a full meal. I don't know how hungry the other guys are, but I hope we can talk things out over some pizza, and maybe we'll begin to feel better after doing so. We walk from the intense cold to a welcoming heated restaurant. A young woman, who looks to be in her younger twenties, approaches us at the front desk.

"Hi," she says. "How many do we have today?"

"Four," says I.

"Alright! You guys can follow me."

We follow behind her and walk past the bar in the middle of the restaurant. She seats us over by the shaded windows and near some older arcade machines. Thomas and I sit on one side and Chester and Ash sit on the opposite side. The waitress sets down menus on the table for us.

"Can I start you guys off with any drinks," she says.

"Blue Moon, please," Thomas says. I can't help but giggle. Ash and Chester chuckle too. "I'm just kidding. I'll take root beer."

"Okay," the waitress says. "How bout for you?"

She looks at me next with her sweet chocolate eyes.

"Could you actually get us all root beers," says I.

"I mean, if you guys want." We all nod *yes* at the waitress. "Sweet! I'll go and get those for you guys."

The waitress leaves as Thomas watches her gain distance.

"Do you guys think she would've fell for it," he says.

"No way," Chester says. "You don't even look 18 with that baby face of yours!"

"Well, if she knew I played hockey, she might have just slid me one!"

"Okay," Ash says. "He has you there!"

"Hey, Liam," Thomas says. "Why did you get us all root beer?"

"Well, cause they come in a bottle," says I.

"And?"

"And he wants us to look like those sober broken-hearted alcoholics from the movies," says Chester.

We all break out into laughter, Ash on the other hand turns into a hyena with his laugh! Man, I think I'm laughing more at his laugh than the actual joke itself.

"Nah," says I. "I want us to feel like we're all together, you know?"

"We'll always be together," Thomas says. "We all have each other's backs, right?"

"Agreed," Chester says.

"Agreed," Ash says.

The waitress comes around the corner of the bar with both her hands holding the heads of our root beers. She comes over to our table and sets them down. She places a root beer on all of our coasters and pulls out a notepad and pen.

"Are you guys ready to order," she says.

"Yeah," says I. "Two large pepperoni pizzas will do."

"Alright, sounds good! I can take your guys' menus." We hand her our menus. She leaves.

"Guys," says I. "Can I ask you something?" They just look at me with no response, but I take it as a yes anyway. "I think I know why Finn was so depressed."

"Do we have to talk about this?" Thomas says.

"Yes! We have to talk about this."

"Go ahead," Chester says.

"So, after the game last night, did you guys notice Finn's face?"

"Yeah," Chester says. "He got beat up."

"Who do you think beat him up?"

"One of the Scythes players, probably in one of those fights."

"No. He didn't get into any fight on the ice."

"What are you trying to say," Ash says.

"On the bus ride home from the game, Finn hopped seats to sit next to me. He said coach abused him for being an embarrassment to the team that night."

"That doesn't make any sense," Thomas says.

"What do you mean?" says I.

"Why would coach care? It's literally the first game of the season."

"Well, since we played bad, it makes HIM look bad."

"And coach only has hope in his first liners," Ash says. He takes a chug of the root beer.

"That's so fucking stupid," Chester says. "They're not even that good!"

"I know," says I. "It's because coach has been friends with all of their fricken parents."

"Well, and they score more goals then you guys," Thomas says.

"The reason why we can't score more goals is because we never get a chance!"

"And don't forget how we never get to play on power plays," Ash says.

"And who gets all the fucking penalties," Chester says. "The first liners do!"

"Guys, guys, guys," says I. "We need to turn coach in for child abuse."

"Woah, woah, woah," Thomas says. "Slow down! We are not turning him in."

"What?"

"Do you know what's going to happen when we don't have a coach again?"

"We'll just find a new coach, and everything will be fine!"

"Liam, it doesn't work that way!"

"Why? Why doesn't it work?"

"You tell me who's going to apply for the coaching position. The school won't let a parent coach the team and there's no other teachers that will. It was hard enough for them to find Kipp."

"We can find someone!"

"Liam, no. It's too risky!"

"He has a point," Ash says. "Liam, it's our senior year of high school. This is our last year of high school hockey! Well, Chester and Thomas still have another year."

He proves a challenging point to me. Once high school hockey is done, there's no going back to it. Hockey is life here in Minnesota, and we'd be willing to do anything to play high school hockey. I sit there, wanting to cry for Finn, but if I turn coach in for child abuse, we might never be able to find a suitable coach for the job, and then our season would be over, and my friends would probably see me as a traitor. Finding a coach in the middle of a court case would take up the whole damn season. Plus, most of Finn's body is frozen and no one could tell that the black eyes were from punches or what the lashes were from. They would've believed it's all from frostbite and it naturally formed onto his body. Then, coach would be denied from the court case, and I'd be sat for the rest of the season. The hockey parents would hate me, and my mother would never look at me the same.

This whole situation is just a mess! Coach doesn't play our line because he only wants to play the popular guys and doesn't want to embarrass himself. The first liners hate our line for whatever secret grudges they have against us. The hockey parents always gossip in the stands about each other's kids. There's just the greatest grain of salt on our team and no one can seem to find it. Everybody is so worried about their social status these days. Sometimes, it just kills me.

ELEVATE

There's nothing like the smell of rubber and stale sweat on a dull Monday morning. We're all supposed to be in the gym every other day before the school bell rings, but only a few of us actually show up. Chester works out during his strength and conditioning class and Ash goes to Snap Fitness on his own time. The great thing is that Ben doesn't show up. It's usually just Jake, Charlie, Thomas, and myself. Once in a while, Finn would come to the gym, but he never really liked Mr. Z, our strength coach.

Mr. Z is a gigantic, built-up steel body of armor. He coaches the football team but manages the weight room in our school. I love Mr. Z! He always tells me how much of a hard worker I am. I believe he's the only one that actually recognizes how much work I put into hockey, and my physical fitness of course. Personally, weightlifting is not exciting, and I barely get any improvement from it, but coaches love to see their athletes working towards a goal.

Old-school rock music blasts from bulky speakers hanging on the wall. The speakers don't have any bass to them, but I guess with rock music, it doesn't really matter. Rock music isn't my cup of coffee for the morning, I'm more of an EDM person myself, but never ask Mr. Z to change the music. Nobody likes the music I listen to anyways. Everybody else in this generation wants to listen to that rap crap where all they sing about is disgusting drugs, gang shootings, and money. That's all Ben plays in the locker room. How are we ever supposed to get electrified before a game with an annoying, repetitive rap beat? At least Mr. Z's taste of music wants to make me whip metal weightlifting plates at the concrete wall to release my mysterious anger that builds inside of me.

Thomas, Jake, and Charlie walk through the door and into the weightlifting room. I always feel left out because it seems nobody wants to have a long conversation with me, even my best friends! As much as I can care less about being by myself and staying outside of the high school drama, it would be nice to talk once in a while.

"Alright, boys," Mr. Z says. "Let's get to work!"

This week is max-out week. Thomas and I will be maxing out on bench, the best upper body workout there is.

"Do you wanna go first?" Thomas says.

"I think you should go first," says I. "You'll have less plates than me."

"That's true."

Thomas puts on a forty-five and I mimic him from the other

side, sliding the cold metal plate on the stainless-steel bar. I look back over to Thomas as he slides on a ten, and I do as well. He locks up the plates on his side and I lock up the plates on my side. I wiggle in between the two bench stands sitting back to back to each other and prepare to spot Thomas. He sits down on the folded chair and swings his arms into a windmill. As he stretches his arms out, I look to see where Jake and Charlie bench. I can see them through one of the skinny little windows in the middle dividing wall. The wall has four windows and it's meant to divide the room for a more organized look, and to make it more functional.

Thomas' body lays back on the seat as his hands grip the steel bar. He squeezes the bar to feel for the little goosebumps and finds good placement for a strong grip. With a strong inhale of air, he pushes up on the bar and brings it over his hefty chest. My hands are near the bar in case he needs the support, but I have faith in him! I will motivate him till the veins inside of his skin pull each other into tense rubber bands. He takes a deep breath in, loading his weapon of choice, drops the bar down to his chest, and then, boom! He fires his strength away from his body, exhaling a gust of Mount Everest's blazing wind, pushing away the rocks that have tumbled before him. The boulder is almost off of him, but he needs to push himself before his muscles collapse into little twigs. My fingertips barely touch the bar as he pushes off with one last spark of energy. Thomas maxes out at 145 pounds.

"Well," Thomas says. "That was fun."

Now, it's my turn. We take the locks off the sides, taking off the ten-pound plate and adding on another forty-five pounds to both sides of the bar. My max goal is to lift 225 pounds and beat my record of 215. I lay down on the hard rubber seat and dangle my arms next to me. I prepare my mind for the challenge to come forth. The music fades out from my ears and my vision focuses on my hands. They float up to the bar and glue themselves shut on the goosebump-grips. Before I can even take a breath, Thomas pulls the weight off its stand. The 225 pounds hovers above me, but I must drop before my arms snap. I take a deep breath like I'm about to go underwater for the longest time of my life, and then I drop the bar towards my chest. With all my might, I explode with energy and push the bar away from me, but from the side of my eye, another person stands by me. I push till my arms lock up and then set the bar back on its shelf. My arms flop down to the sides while I look over to find Mr. Z.

"Look at you," he says. "I wish you were on the football team!"

I chuckle at his joke, not knowing how to respond because he knows I don't like the sport. But the team is awful with the players being scrawnier than the dead branches on the winter trees.

"What is that, 225?" he says.

"Yep," says I.

"Liam, I think you're on the leaderboard!"

"Is he really?" Thomas says.

"Let's go find out."

Mr. Z walks us out onto the track that sits above both basketball courts. The leaderboard hangs on the wall right outside of the weightlifting room. It lists bench, clean, and squats, and I have already made the leaderboard for squats and clean. My maxed-out squat is 420 pounds and my clean was not the best, mainly because it's such an awkward motion of sticking your arms out like flamingo legs.

"Yep," Mr. Z says. "You made it, son!"

"Oh my God," Thomas says. "You're fucking strong, dude!"

"I try sometimes," says I.

Just the perfect time too, Coach Kipp approaches us on the track.

"What do we have goin on here," he says.

"Liam here benched a two twenty-five!"

"Wow! We got some strong muscles on the team!"

"I wish he played football! We can use some stronger men."

"I think Liam's going to be great playing first line next game."

"That he is!"

No way! Am I seriously playing on the first line? This is amazing! Maybe the tides are finally turning, not the way I dreamt it to happen though.

"Big game this Tuesday," Mr. Z says.

"Dorcha," coach says.

"Haven't defeated that team in years."

"That coach pisses me off every time I look at his scrunched-up raccoon face," says I.

"That's the spirit," coach says. "We need you boys to show up tomorrow!"

THE PENALTY

In my past two years, Dorcha has been our archnemesis. They always like to make fun of the Knights and how they're weak with all that armor on, but what they don't know is the strength we have under our feet. Maybe, we can win a game if I show up at my finest. A big pasta feed would be amazing tonight before the big game. Dorcha is an hour drive away, and that's a great time to listen to all of my warmup songs. Awe! I'm too excited for this moment! Finally, it's my turn to shred up the ice!

LAKE OF THE WOODS

My anxiety escalates inside of an elevator, starting from my stomach and building up to my beating heart. The gears of excitement and fear twist with unexplainable energy. Coach Kipp writes our lineups for practice on the board with a black whiteboard marker. I can sense the expo marker from my stall, and Ben can too. He stares at the board while coach leaves the room. I watch him, waiting for a deceiving glance from his eyes to peer into mine. The rest of the team looks at the lineups, looking for what color they'll be wearing. It's not like it matters though, the lines have always been the same throughout high school. Sometimes, coach will randomly switch the first liners from white jerseys to black, and vice versa, but it doesn't make any difference in the end.

Ben stops looking at the board and slides his skates on. Our line wears white today, and I hope I have white socks. Nothing causes me more anxiety then missing a pair of socks before practices and games. I stand up and dig through my cubby for my white socks. As I look into my cubby, I can see him from the side of my eye. Now, he finally peers over at me. I can work straight through the pepper right now and find his one grain of salt. It doesn't take a genius to find the dry, salty desert within him.

I slide on my white socks, pull up my bulky breezers, and lace on my skates. Then, I put on my chest and elbow pads. Apparently, I put on my elbow pads backwards because Danny always gives me shit about it. He seems to forget how many times he mentions it to everyone on the team. But I like sliding my elbow pads on this way, I've been doing it like this for years. Also, the velcro on my elbow pads would always detach when I had them on the "correct" way. Elbow pads have never been comfortable in my eyes, but they are now. So, I'll slide my elbow pads on my arm any way the fuck I want.

Once I throw on my white practice jersey, I grab my helmet from the top shelf and snap on the chin and side buckles. As I grab my gloves and walk over to the stick stand, the clicking of my skates pluck every vein inside Ben. I just walk past him, holding my head high and being my settled self. I search for my hockey stick on the stick stand and find it with its chipped-up tape job. Puck marks splatter the white tape on my nicked-up blade. With the room filling up with a questionable chemical disaster, I leave it in its awkward environment.

The elongated hallway. Wall colors of grey and white are split along on a maroon stripe. Players from this community in the past have walked down this hall, all the way to the Minnesota

State Hockey Tournament. This has always been a dream of mine as a hockey player; warming up in the Wild's Xcel Energy Center, skating in front of thousands of seats and fans from around the state, EDM music pumping through the stadium and the television cameras streaming live. What a great experience to have as a high schooler.

I click my skates past the coach's locker room when I hear a door shut from behind me. Chester exits the room and follows me to the french doors. I open the doors and walk on the rubber mats to the sheet of ice. The zamboni resurfaces the ice as I skate across to the benches. When I hop myself onto the bench and sit on the boards, Chester skates onto the ice and sits next to me. I swish-swash my stick in the puddled water that soaks up the ice under my feet. Hopefully, it's not one of those days where the water takes decades to freeze. The only thing the water would freeze then is the puck from sliding across the ice, but I shouldn't complain while there is a warm and loving soul covered-up from beneath.

The zamboni completes its laps around the ice. That's when everyone else on the team steps on, including coach who follows behind them. I hop off the boards and onto the ice. In the beginning of practice, I like to skate around at a decent pace and shred up the ice a bit with crossovers. Cole and Thomas take the leaning nets off the boards and set them up in their crease. They bang the pegs into the ice and lift the nets on top of them. That's when the fireflies get a spark of energy in them. All the forwards and defensemen, including me, steals a puck from the pile and quickly takes top-shelfer shots at the net. Usually, a lot of pucks miss the net, bang off the glass, and slide to the side for me to pick up another one.

Coach blares a quick peep of the whistle. It's time to skate some warmup laps. I take quick hard steps into the ice and transition into longer strides to keep my speed up. I skate to the outside of the net with quick crossovers, watching as the rest of the team cuts corners and laps around the neutral zone.

Another peep of the whistle from the coach and we take a steady coast on the ice. Danny dangles with a puck in his hands and Ben fires a wrist shot at the net. Coach blows his whistle and we lap the ice again. I keep my push within me and work hard around the net building up speed. As I come around the net and up the boards into a sprinting runaway, Ben cuts me off and slows my speed down.

Peep! I take slow strides as I coast around the outside of the net again. The next whistle blows and I turn on my boost. I dig up the ice with my blades and full-out sprint the length of the ice. I pass coach who skates like his muscles are shriveling up, slowly skating around the center of the ice. He starts off by bending his legs and pushing off the ice with hard strides, but then he stands straight and coasts, watching the rest of us circle around him. But man, it feels great flying by him like a fighter pilot jet in the murkiness of World War II.

The coach gives three chirps of the whistle and we all skate to the center of the ice. We kneel on the red outline of the faceoff dot and stretch our legs out into taffy. Coach stands in the middle of us as he unwraps a sheet of paper, listing the drills we are working on today. I don't know why he wastes paper though; the drills never change. It does give the impression that he knows what he's doing.

"Alright, boys," says coach. "Today is going to be short. We're going to start off with Lake of the Woods, work on breakouts and offensive zone, and then play a small scrimmage of Gretzky in the end."

Thank God! Practice kind of sucks after an exhausting seven-hour day of school. School just sucks the energy out of us, shoving seven different subjects into our heads every day. It's great to give our brains a break and to give our muscles some rest before the big game. Full-on conditioning before games is the worst plan ever. Work us hard today like you want us to work tomorrow, but that doesn't make sense. We use all our energy today, then we won't have that same energy tomorrow, because we used it all fucking today! Get that through your head, coaches! Save that energy, and let it build more tension in our blood. We will explode our energy tomorrow when it's the real deal. Practice is meant to work on skills that need improvement. We will worry about your physical status on our own, we're old enough to do so. Well, at least some of us on the team understand that concept. Danny drinks pop every day during school, which explains why he drinks all of the water from the bottles during practices.

With another peep of the whistle, we group into three lines on the red line near the goalie's net, spreading out across the width of the rink. Ben is on the centerline with Ash behind him, Danny and

Chester are on their right-wing post, and I'm all alone on my left-wing post. This is going to be more playing time than I've ever expected to have. Butterflies paint circles in my stomach as I stand in line, waiting for the commander to signal us. I bend my knees and prepare my feet to kick the ice back from under me. Ben has the puck on his stick, ready to pass it to me or Danny.

Peep! I push off the ice as Ben takes a couple hard shreds. He skates to the blue line and angles to pass the puck to Danny. Danny retrieves the puck on the blade of his stick. He takes a few more strides before passing it to me, throwing it across the neutral zone and hitting my stick around the far blue line. Now, it's time to loop back around to our lines. I hold the puck and skate it down to the opposite zone, but when we loop around, do I go on the inside of Danny and Ben, or do I stay on the outside? If I make the wrong choice, I could end up colliding with one of them, embarrassing myself and building coach's rage. He would explode and impale us with his anger, ready to skate us for the rest of practice.

Focus, Liam, focus! I skate on the outside rim as Ben flows with my direction, skating back up the ice on my side. Danny crosses the width of the ice. As Ben and I loop back up the ice together, I hand the puck up to Ben's stick. He skates the puck into the zone where the next line stands, giving Danny a pass and ending with a slapshot on the open net. Cole and Thomas don't have to be a part of this drill. They work on their own skills down on the other end of the ice with crease work.

This is going to be rough. Luckily, Charlie and Jake are here to jump in line. They don't play forward positions, but they're reasonable to help me out. Jake goes with my old line as a left winger, and Charlie stays back in the centerman line. I get back into my empty line and catch my breath before the next peep of the whistle.

Shockingly, everything went smooth as cool whip with me, Ben, and Danny. How in the world did we manage to do that? This is the first time that I've ever skated on their line, and we actually got something accomplished. But that's only because coach insists that we follow the drill's rule: everyone must touch the puck.

In a hockey game, Ben and Danny are going to be puck hogs, holding each other's hand to failure.

BLACK ICE

Sweat drips off my curly hair and trickles down my acne-filled face. The great potency of our hard work humidifies the locker room. Chester is already taking off his bottom halves as I'm unbuckling my helmet straps. He's a fricken concord ripping through his gear. I don't blame him for wanting to get out of this soaking gear. The other guys take their time and chit chat to one another. I sit down inside of my stall and pull off my jersey and upper body pads. Coach walks in through the door as I quickly unlace my double-knotted skates. Coaches don't like it when players take their gear off as they talk to us, presenting their very informative speeches. He grabs a whiteboard from the front of the room and sits on a black fold-up chair by the stick stand.

"How ya boys feeling?" coach says.

"Good," Ben says.

Coach's lips hesitate to say something. He's so awkward sometimes. The train inside his head loses its grip on the rails from time to time, and I know it makes him a little furious on the inside.

"Dorcha," coach says. "One of our biggest games of the year. The Dragons have three lines. The first line is the most dangerous line on the team. They have two D1 commits who will be a challenge to get the puck through. They're both gigantic defenseman who'll try to knock you off the puck by their blue line, so keep your head up! This team likes to play hardcore offense, and it won't be easy to get around them, but you guys need to show up tomorrow and rip the game right out from their hands. No one will be expecting it. Don't you guys just want to show them up?"

I'm not going to lie, that would be the best thing to happen this year. The Dragons have always been a disrespectful team to us, and I will not stand and get bashed with their arrogant insults. They think their team has so much more skill than we do, but it's funny to think we only have two lines and we can keep them within a two-goal difference all the time!

"The bus leaves at 3:30 tomorrow, after school," coach says. "Make sure you boys stay hydrated and eat a good meal tonight."

Coach leaves the locker room.

"Boys!" Ben says. "Team meal at Upside!"

"Wooooooooo!" Danny says.

It's doesn't take a pop of a weasel to know Danny would cheer about food. All he does is pound down pop during the day and loads himself with fatty foods later on. He's always out of shape, which explains why he moves into a slow dance during some of our games, if not all of them.

"Hey," Chester says. "Are you going to Upside?"

"No," says I.

"Me neither!"

Chester chuckles out a laugh for the both of us. We both know what we'd have to deal with. If we were to show up and take a seat at the same table with them, they would ignore us the whole time. They probably wouldn't even know what to talk about. All they want to talk about is their saltiness towards me, moving up to their line. It'd just be an awkward breakfast of bavardage. Plus, I don't even feel accepted to join them.

"I have to work today too," says I.

"Oh dang," Chester says.

I slide on my shoes, which are like a mix between hiking shoes and athletic shoes. I throw on my hockey sweatshirt and my beanie hat. It's probably not even blistering cold outside, but it still sucks when sweat freezes to the skin.

"See ya later," says I.

"See ya tomorrow!"

The endless hallway. Another stroll down the long hall takes me pass the empty dryland room. I turn the corner into the warming area, but a pair of footsteps grows louder and louder into my ears like tree roots delving into the soil in search for water. It feels like someone is chasing down the hallway to grab me from behind or something. The steps stomp the rubber floors of the hallway, vibrating the rubber beneath the soles of my feet. My heart bounces and rebounds my anxiety with every tick of the wall clock. The concession stand is closed, and the rink manager is resurfacing the ice. I'm all alone, but the sunset shimmers off the snow-covered ground through the front doors of the rink. I hurry myself over to the door when I find myself halting from leaving The Barn.

"Liam," Danny says.

"What's up," says I.

"Are you going to Upside with us?"

"I want to, but I have to go to work."

"You too?"

"Yeah. You work tonight?"

"Well, I'm scheduled too, but I'm going to ask Kiv if he can cover."

"Yeah, I'm sure he'll be fine with it. The rink is going to be quiet tonight anyways."

"Yeah, hopefully."

"Alright, I should get goin. See ya tomorrow!"

"Yep."

I push myself out the door and into the cold. It strikes my head with a brain freeze as I shuffle my feet across the black ice in the parking lot. I pull out my keys and hop into my vehicle. The seat is cold, and my breath fogs up the windshield. I twist the key in the ignition, and immediately, I turn on the seat warmers and crank the heat to high. Safety first, gotta buckle up with all this black ice hiding on the roads. Black ice is the most terrifying hazards on the winter roads.

Black ice hides. Black ice waits. Black ice cripples. It's torture knowing that it awaits for someone's fate, but if you're careful, slow, and really focus on the road in front of you, then you are more likely to arrive at your destination.

I back out of the parking space and drive to the 30mph road. My radio is silently turned on, and I spin the volume wheel to increase the sound. A Christmas song ends as the talkman's voice overlays the fading music.

"It's a cold day out there! Temperatures average around zero degrees across the state with the northwest breeze dropping the wind chill to negative six. There's a frost advisory set for 10pm that will last through tomorrow morning. A winter storm watch has been issued for several counties around the metro as heavy moisture moves into our region tomorrow evening. The storm is expected to produce up to a foot of snow overnight and will carry a few more inches into Wednesday morning. Temperatures will continue to plummet later in the week. Stay cozy, folks!"

Currently, the winter sun peeks over the horizon line at 5:30pm. It's a good thing I work as a lifeguard. Our indoor community pool lives in its sticky tropics and the hot tub is a natural hot spring for my legs. This job doesn't pay much, but I do love how community pools stay peaceful in the winter. No swimming lessons tonight, which is the absolute best! It'll be a simple, cozy day on the job.

Tonight, I work the night shift with my all-time best friend, Marie. Her and I always talk about the beauty of our elementary childhood. We grew up having the same exact teachers and classes together from kindergarten through fifth grade! We support each other no matter what because we deeply care about each other. We care to always keep our strong, healthy harmony with each other and to always be there when one of us falls down into a gorge.

Our lead lifeguard for the night is Treena, and she's great. The best thing about lifeguarding at this pool is the friends and the community I get to work with. They make the job exciting and enjoyable, even the managers are awesome. But every job has its flaws once in a while. Some of the teens who swim here don't obey the rules that are posted on gigantic posters that literally span the size of a jumbotron, and parents don't always watch their young ones, thinking their lifejackets are going to keep them safe from any tragic event. Many customers stamp their complaints on the front desks' face, complaining about the prices of daily admissions or upset about our pool not having punch cards anymore. Whatever it is, there'll always be the considerate and there will always be the cynical.

I arrive at the pool and park my SUV in the lower employee lot. The car snugs me in its heat that finally kicks in, but the thought of the hot tub motivates me to prop my door open. The cold breeze pushes the heat out of my vehicle as I throw on my backpack, shut the door, and walk the cold concrete steps to the front doors. Six glass doors span a wide entrance to the newly built community center. Walking in, you approach the front desk, and on the left are the double set of french doors to the pool. Before moving inside the tropical humidity, pizza swirls through the air from the concession stands, which sits on the left prior to the pool doors. No customer ordered a pizza, I just know it. The concession stand worker is bored and hungry as hell. That's the plodding position as the night slithers like a nightcrawler.

When I open the doors, the heat moistens my body. I walk down a flight of stairs to the pool deck. A huge length of bleachers layers the right side of the lap pool. The 50,000-ton bulkhead sits in the center of the pool, used as a divider to split the lap swimmers from the diving boards and the rock climbing walls in the deep end. That bulkhead is the most spine-chilling thought in this entire pool. The dangers of a kid swimming under the bulkhead paralyzes my thoughts of watching the deep end. They can swim under the portable bulkhead and get stuck underneath it. Kids can drown under the bulkhead without anyone even realizing it. You definitely need to keep your eyes glued to the water at all times.

A wall to my left is where the locker rooms are located. I walk down half the width of the lap pool and a kiddy pool appears in the back-left corner. The kiddy pool is a pain with the mushroom waterfalling a sheet of frosted glass. No lifeguard will ever like the mushroom because it obstructs our view of the young patrons in the water. The kids also love to step on the geysers and see how high the water will launch, and sometimes, it surprisingly has enough pressure to soak the ceiling. One of the most tedious things with the kiddy pool has to be the small slide. Little ones don't understand the concept of a slide. You slide down a slide, you don't climb up one, especially when it's fricken slick! Connected to the kiddy pool is also a shallow water-walking loop, which is mainly meant for the elders.

Treena sits on the tiled bench near the kiddy pool, watching a young mother play with her daughter in the mushroom's waterfall. I give a quick wave at her as I turn to the right after the lap pool. Our lifeguard room is basically a storage room placed right next to the hot tub. The room holds all of the swimming instructor's gear like floaties, goggles, toys, and also our chemicals and first aid that we need to regulate on a daily basis. I walk inside and find Marie doing math homework on the small break table.

"Hey," says I.

"What's up?" she says.

"How's work been?"

"Slow."

"Yeah, I don't expect much on a Monday."

I scan my finger on the digital sign-in sheet. It's quite convenient to have for a community swimming pool in a small town. Honestly, this community center almost seems a bit too modern for my taste. All of the floors and walls in this pool are covered in white and light blue tiles. There's barely any color in here but the blasting bright white.

"Do you wanna take Treena for me?" she says.

"Yes. I can do that."

I scavenge through my backpack and pull out my lifeguard trunks and shirt. Behind Marie, I pull off my sweatpants, hockey sweatshirt, shirt, socks, and lift my swim trunks over my underwear. I throw my lifeguard shirt on and grab a red lifeguard tube. These tubes bend like taffy and it blows my mind how useful they are when you have to make a save in the water.

Treena chills on the bench as I stroll on over to cover her

position. "Aye yo!"

"Hey," she says.

"How are you doing?"

"Good! How bout you?"

"Pretty good! Just got done with hockey."

"Nice!"

"I've heard it's been slow all day."

"Yeah. Just a few lap swimmers came in, and this mother and her child have been in here for a while. Wouldn't be surprised if they leave soon."

"Are you doing half hour rotations?"

"Yeah."

"Okay. Cool beans."

"Imma go have some trail mix. I'm starving."

"Don't make me hungry now!"

She leaves to the lifeguard room. The mother watches her daughter take her hand through the sheet of the waterfall. The little girl's amusement of the water is so precious to watch. She giggles while the water from her hand sprays in the direction of her mom. The water only sprays along her thighs as the little girl looks to be small like a four-year-old. A pink life jacket is buckled onto her, which makes me feel quite comfortable.

The mother walks out from under the mushroom waterfall. She walks out of the pool to her beach bag sitting on the bench to the right of me. I turn my vision back to her daughter, sitting down in the water under the mushroom top. I can barely notice her fingers twiddling through the water as the waterfall slams against the surface of the pool, splashing the water around the mushroom's radius.

The mother sits on the bench wrapped in a towel and scrolls through her phone. I wonder if she knows the rule about kids under six in the swimming pool. Nah, it's not a big deal. They're the only ones here and I can deal with one calm kid. It doesn't harm anything. Besides, I'm enjoying my time sitting here as much as the two of them are here. The waterfall is quite loud but pleases my mind with the constant rush of splashing water. The little girl's joyful voice satisfies my eyes in happiness as she swishes her hands in the water.

My manager appears from behind the wall and passes the kiddy pool. She waves at me and peers at the little girl. Oh no! Keep walking, please keep on walking! I know what she's thinking, and I guess I should do something about it. She walks to her office next to the lifeguard room. Should I say something to the mom? I mean, maybe she's fine with it, but what if she isn't? I don't want her to stroll on over and do my job for me, that's embarrassing! Oh my God, I don't know what to do. Stop shaking your leg, Liam! Just be strong and ask the mother in a polite manner. Nope, it's too late. She just answered a call.

Nice. Now what? Her little kid waddles her little duck feet over to the slide, and they aren't waddling to the stairs. Don't you even think about climbing up that slide, missy! I'd really appreciate it if you wouldn't force me to do my job! I see your little hands touching the bottom of that slide. Don't you dare spider crawl up that slick slide. There's not a chance you will make it to the top going up this way. Fuck! She's doing it. Hey, mom, stop talking on the phone and watch your child. I hope my manager doesn't leave her room right now. Can the thumping of my heart and the flow of my blood slow down please? This is too much. Oh my, she's climbing the slide. Thud! The little girl slides down to the rubber padding below . . . She's going to try it again, isn't she?

I glance at the mother again, she's looking at her child climbing up the slide, but doesn't show a hint in her movements to take any necessary action. She's deep into her conversation with whoever the hell she's talking to. Is she stupid or something? Your kid is going to hurt herself one of these times, especially since she's attempting to walk up the slide this time. Okay, I don't need any trouble for not doing my duty. I walk collectively over to the waterslide and set my tube on the slide, blocking off her path to a chaotic injury.

"Hey, sweetie," says I. "You can't go up the slide. You only go down the slide, okay?"

She rolls down the slide and sits on the rubber platform. Her cute green googly eyes bulge out at me in confusion. I hope she can understand what I'm trying to say. I turn around to walk to the side of the pool, walking knee deep in the water. The mother watches her daughter with me as she proceeds to talk on her phone. I sit on the edge platform with my feet dangling in the water as the little girl hops back onto her feet and attempts the slide again.

Ugh! This girl is a little tedious gnat who purposely wants to annoy the living daylight out of my soul. I walk back to the slide and block it with my rubber tube for the second time. She stops and looks at me.

"No," says I.

I remove my tube from the slide and slowly back away. She lifts her left foot and sets it on the slide. You have to be fucking kidding me! No! No! No! I spin around to the mother and she just looks at me with her relaxed, green eyes.

"Excuse me, mam," says I.

"One second, honey," she says, putting down the phone. "Yes?"

"You need to be in the water with her."

"We're leaving here soon."

"Well that's fine, but she needs to come out of the water if you're not in there with her."

"Why do I have to be in there?"

"It's a rule here. Children under six need a parent or guardian in the water with them at all times."

She sets her phone down on the bench and walks over to her daughter, still attempting to climb up that annoying slide. She picks her up and heads to the locker room with her items. Finally, they're gone! With a big breath, I flush out the anxiety from my system and wander back to the lifeguard room.

"Oh my God," says I. "That kiddy slide is the most annoying thing ever."

"Was the girl trying to climb it?" Treena says.

"Yes! Constantly, over and over again. I told her three times to stop while her mother just sat on her phone."

"Was she out of the water?"

"Yes!"

"Cause I had to tell her the rule that she needs to stay in the water with her kid."

"She clearly didn't get the memo. I had to tell her to go in the water with her kid too, but she said they were leaving and stormed out."

"Well, now we don't have to worry about her."

"Until next time. It just annoys me how a mother can't take the responsibility to care for her own child! That little girl would've gotten hurt if it wasn't for me. And, of course, I probably look like the bad guy!"

WOLF ATTACK

Wolves. Their fur is as soft as vanilla custard, so precious and
delicate to the touch. I wrap myself within the browns and greys,
keeping myself tucked in from the morning light. There's
something about wolves that inspires me. They stand tall on a
cliff's edge, ready to conquer any mountain that stands in their
way. They are introverts who aren't scared of predators. A wolf's
call blows a cool breeze through the pines, warning their predators
that they are on their way to feast, but yet the calls are pleasing to
the ear like the plush pillow pressing against mine.

Wolves focus their golden eyes to a reasonable aperture,
maybe targeting a red fox scavenging through the three-foot snow.
Their desire and want for a meal intensifies their focus on their
goal of success. Food, they need food to survive the starch winter,
so nothing is stopping them. The wolf zooms in on the red fox and
darts through the white fluff. Its steps markup the snow, but the
white fluff soothes the galloping paws as it targets the red fox. The

wolf's teeth rip the fox into the air and shakes it like a slobbery chew toy. The fox's blood melts the snow into a scrumptious cherry snow cone. Now, the fox is dead, and the wolf munches its chewy and slimy remains, digesting it into its slushy stomach.

Another wolf leaps out from the surrounding pines. Its milky teeth widens into a vigorous growl. Wolves self-care, and when they don't receive what they want, it turns into one messy dog fight. One wolf leaps for the other as they jab their claws into one another. One claw takes its nails and carves a bleeding scar into the wolf's white and brown fur. The brisk air seeps through the fur and sinks down into the scar.

"Liam," a woman's voice says. "Time to wake up."

I find my warm pelt pulled off of my body as the overcast day shines through the window and upon my mother, standing next to my bed.

"Breakfast should be done soon! You have a big game today! Get dressed and you can come down and eat."

She walks out and closes the door behind her. The morning air chills my bones with goosebumps raising the hair on my legs. I swing my legs to the side of the bed, lifting my chest up with slouching shoulders and sleepy eyes. I walk over to my drawers and scavenge for a clean pair of game day sweats. My pants slide on my legs, heating them like a fireplace on Christmas Eve, warming the house with love. I go inside of my closet and throw over an athletic shirt and my game day sweatshirt.

I walk out of the closet and back into the settled light that shines through the cold dead windows. The hefty snowstorm is probably building out there in the Dakotas. The trees outside calmly nestle in the hushed environment. There's always a moment of silence before all hell breaks loose.

As I walk towards my bedroom door and open it, I take a few steps before looking up and finding myself in the excruciating long hallway in The Barn. A boy dressed in a black wind jacket, black wind pants, and a black beanie hat stands at the far end of the hallway. He stands there dead as a scarecrow, staked into the ground and staring in this direction. My body shocks in stillness as my legs lock up and my shoulders tighten. My eyes directly focus on his blackholed-eyes, but I can't clearly see him, he's so far back. A strong brush of wind pushes through my locked body, and the sound of rushing waves echoes through the hallway.

A redwater wave flows around the corner and crashes into the wall. The redwater curls over the boy's head and crashes onto the other wall. The wave splashes onto him, but he stands in place. He didn't move a single muscle. Redwater floods the hall like it's in a lower living quarters of a sinking ship. The redwater crawls its way and touches our locker room door. The boy's head drowns in the flood. I find my thoughts sinking back into my brain. I take a deep breath as my legs loosen and my shoulders relax. Before the wave crashes into me, I turn around and sprint into my room. I spin around again as the redwater wave approaches my door, but I slam the door in time, sealing the letter inside its envelope. My body flushes against the door and slides down to the carpet.

"Liam," my mother says. "Liam, are you awake?"

A quick second of silence passes as I hear footsteps vibrating the floor from the hallway. I jump straight into my bed, wrap myself in the fur, and seal my eyes shut. A couple of knocks, then the door opens.

"Time to get up, Liam! You have school soon."

"Sorry," says I. "I'll be down in sec."

"Did you get a good sleep?"

"Yeah."

"Come on down. Your breakfast is ready."

She walks back downstairs leaving my door open this time. I hop out of bed and peer down the hallway. It's back to the dark dusty hallway it's always been. I stroll down the hallway and down the steps. A huge whiff of pancakes swirls through my nose as I enter the kitchen. My mother has a plate of pancakes and a glass of milk on the table for me. She sits next to my chair, taking a bite from her pancake and looking up to find my eyes. Her hand pats the chair next to her as she sneaks a smile at me. I sit down in my chair with my legs out to the side. I angle my chest towards the kitchen while I pick up my fork and take a chunk of a buttery pancake.

"How's the pancakes," she says.

"Good," says I.

"Every athlete needs a great breakfast before their big game! Dorcha's gonna be tough!"

She takes another bite of her pancake, as so do I. I latch my attention on the pancakes in front of me, soaking in a sweet but bitter maple syrup.

"I heard you're playing first line tonight," she says.

"Yep," says I.

"Ash's parents told me last night. They're happy coach moved you up."

"Yeah. I wish he would move our whole line up."

"Yeah, that's what I said to Ash's parents."

I chow down the last pieces of my pancakes and chug my milk to a brain freeze.

"I gotta get goin," says I.

"Sounds good," she says. "Score some goals tonight."

"I will." Or so I will try.

FEED THE WOLF

My jersey hangs off the side of the window. I lift the bottom of my jersey and shove it in between the seat and the side of the bus, just like the curtains that drape inside our dining room. The cold frosts over the windows on the school bus, smudging my view to the overcast day. The palm of my hand pushes against the frosted window, melting it from under my warm skin. I wave my hand across the window to melt the frost off. Outside, a dark wall cloud pushes over the muddy farm fields.

I lean my head on the glass and watch the yellow lines on the country road. They appear but then dash away like little fireflies, and every dash is one step closer to Dorcha. My headphones pump hardcore dubstep music into my head. Every bass drop kicks an adrenaline rush through my blood. My heart skips beats but pumps the blood through my veins so fast that my legs lighten into feathers, ready to sweep this game away. If I want to make an impression for the team, I must play one hell of a game tonight. I will have my inner wolf prepared to howl our team to victory.

Danny shoves a Dorcha player into the boards. He ties the guy up in our defensive zone, the puck trapped between their battling feet and sticks. I manage to poke the puck with my stick and deflect it off the boards in front of me. My momentum pushes me towards the Dragon's defense as I carry the puck, building speed with vigorous strides. As I approach their blue line, they begin to pressure me to the side of the boards. He wants to hammer my body into the glass and drop me to my feet, but that's not happening today, buddy. I turn on my boosters and flash with insane speed. I shove my shoulder into his waist, pushing him away from the puck that my stick protects. My stick slides across the ice in front of the goalie, heading for the other side of the net. But I pull my stick back and fake the goalie out. His movement follows my movement as my stick fires the puck from behind me. The puck top-shelfs the net with an explosion of excitement from the student section. Someone in the section will be shaking a sign that paints the message *21 is the one*. I keep my composure and skate to the side, my line mates coming in for a group hug. We break the hug, then I lead my guys to our bench for a victorious line of fist bumps with our team.

A bump of the bus catches me off guard. We have arrived. A few Dorcha players walk to the front entrance of their arena, wearing the orange Dragon jackets. One of the guys wears a beanie hat over his black shaggy hair. His skin is pale white, and his nose reddens from the cold. He wears skinny athletic sweatpants that look exactly like mine. He has the same number as me, but his *21* is orange. Gross.

The bus halts in front of the arena's doors. We all stand up from our seats and hurry off. I walk down the stairs with every step burning more cold air on my face. My shoes crunch salt from beneath which scatters the concrete sidewalk. The boys and I open the trailer's back door. Cole obtains his legs pads and his bulky bag from the top of the pile. Ben and Danny throw some bags onto the ground and grab theirs from the back of the trailer. Meanwhile, Ash found his bag on the ground. I look at one of the bags, but there's white hockey tape wrapped around the shoulder strap. Mine doesn't have any tape on it. I discover my bag sitting next to the one with the tape and head inside the rink.

The Dorcha Dragon's arena has nothing unique about it. All hockey rinks in Minnesota are awesome, but I may be a little biased on this one. Thin brown metal supports line the ceiling, orange bleachers pushed tightly against the left side of the ice, and the locker rooms lie right under the bleachers. When locker rooms are located under the bleachers, then you know the rooms are claustrophobic death traps. If we had one more line on our team, we'd be having to split into two separate locker rooms, first liners getting their own room. They'd steal the boombox too, but I shouldn't complain too much. We might as well just load down a cup of depressants into our system before the game and hope for the best. That's why I wear headphones to my games. I listen to real music that electrifies your blood and pumps the heart to the beat.

Banners hang over the Dorcha's logo, which is two dragons

spitting out flames on center ice. One of the banners was from last year's state tournament. The Dragons compete with single A teams which makes their conference much easier than ours. Kielstad moved up to double AA but I never agreed with that decision. Our team is so small, yet our school size seems to have reached the limit of students for the bigger conference. What else is confusing is that the Huskies are basically an undefeated team, reaches to the state tournament every year, and takes first place in the tournament all the time. Clearly, their competition needs to be raised, but the state won't move them to double AA. Instead, let's move the Knights up so they can lose even more games than usual. Sorry, we don't have hockey rinks that stay open 24/7 nor do our families have the money to send us to hockey camps in Canada for the summer. We don't have the gold or the population to be as skilled as the Bumblebees and the Mammoths, and if only we had some true team bonding, maybe that would get us somewhere.

I follow the boys into a cramped tunnel, and we walk inside a confined locker room. The dim lights on the white concrete ceilings depresses the mood, at least rap music has some umph to it. The room is as skinny as our school bus; three benches outline the sides of the walls. I walk to the back corner near Ash and drop my bag next to his. I zip open my bag and rummage through my gear for black tape and scissors. Chester walks into the locker room with his hockey bag and the stick bag. He drops it in the middle of the locker room as the sticks clonk on the floor. Danny immediately jumps up from his seat and obtains his stick. Chester releases his bag as it plonks onto the floor. He sits down with a sigh of fatigue. Ben plugs the boombox into the bottom outlet, his phone plugged into the top. Charlie plays the music from his phone, but I don't hate him for it. He shows strong leadership, but he only plays rap music for the boys, and once in a while he will goof around with them, but what would a team be without a goofy defenseman? Before he plays the colorful language on the boombox, I grab my tape and scissors and prepare to leave the room.

"Chester," says I. "Do you wanna tape your stick on the bleachers with me?"

"I'll be up in a sec," he says.

He hangs his head down at his bag. He doesn't look to be in the mood to talk with anyone. On my way out of the locker room, I grab my hockey stick from the stick bag. I exit the room and walk down the tight hallway. Three Dorcha boys walk towards my direction. They chit chat to each other as I pass them with a grinning face. At the end of the hallway, I turn left and find the stairs to the orange bleachers. I walk to the second highest row of bleachers and choose a spot in the middle of the bench.

My stick's tape job is horribly chipped up from last practice. Luckily, the tape ripped off in one chunk and I don't have to use my short fingernails to claw off the sticky tape. Unlike other hockey players, I don't care to make my tape job look like it's entering into a beauty contest. The tape is there to protect the blade and handle the puck easier. It's not your fricken impression that makes you look good, but it's your hard work ethic that people notice, some just choose not to say anything about it.

Bantam players work on a shooting drill from both sides of the ice. Brings back great memories to the days with the boys. Dad would be coaching our team with great drills and games during practice, and we'd all be loving every little moment with each other. Late night practices were awesome; they really made the end of my day special. Hockey is a spark that lights a flame inside of me and it will never burn out. Another great thing about bantams was all the traveling I got to do with dad; long road trips and weekend layovers up north. We'd stay in hotels and the team would always jump into the pool after the game. A nice dip in the hot tub would relax the sores and bruises from the last hockey game. Nothing can beat the hot chlorinated lava sprouting out from the jets, gently massaging the body.

Danny walks up the steps to the bleachers, followed by Cole and Ben. They sit in the bottom corner near the steps with their hockey sticks and white tape. Of course, they all need to have matching tape color. It'll be the end of the world if they don't have matching wedding rings on their fingers. Ash and Chester walk up the steps together, at least they'll come and sit next to me. They take a seat to the right of me but leave a good gap with Ash's stick resting between us. My noise cancelling headphones squeeze over my ears, the EDM music making the bantam practice more intense. Their feet move like fingers typing away a novel on a typewriter. They stickhandle the puck with a one-on-one competition against a defenseman. A few of the players show off their dangles, and others focus on speed, rushing to the net like they see someone who's going to get crushed by an inattentive double-decker London bus. It's awesome to see kids sweating puddles on the ice, but I know most of them are doing it for show in front of the high school players and coaches. They know they need to look good to make their future high school team, but once they make it, some don't realize that the passionate work ethic has to continue. Just because you made the varsity team doesn't mean you can sit back and slack off.

I get ready to head down to the locker room after taping my stick, but there seems to be an anomalous red glow from the left side of the bleachers. My vision is directed to the heaters that dangle above the Dragon's seating area. The scorching but yet pleasant heat shines its vivant red to my eyes, torturing me as I sit in the unpleasant cold of the arena. The flaring heater burns my vision from afar. It's strange how the heaters are only turned on in their section. The heaters barely sway above me with their dark, frigid metal exterior. Chills shiver down the back of my spine and up through my legs. Goosebumps tickle my arms as I stand on the bleachers. My head seems to lose balance with a sensation of lightheadedness. Maybe I need to drink more water before it's game time.

Down the bleachers I pass the boys and back into the cramped tunnel. Thomas bounces a ball off the wall near the locker room door, swiping it away with his gloved hand. A few of our backup sticks stand against the wall in the hallway, the stick bag lying on the floor next to them. I sneak by Thomas like a mouse and head inside the locker room. The vacancy is quite peaceful. No one's around to bother my concentration for the game. Spoke too soon.

Coach Kipp pushes the door open. "What's happenin?"

I pause my music and slide my headphones down around my neck. "Nothin much."

"Ready for the big game?"

"Always ready, coach."

He sneaks a smirk with those dry, peeling lips of his. Coach stares me down as I sit on the bench across the room, but I focus my vision on my hockey bag. With slight movement from the top of my eyelids, he relocates his attention to the whiteboard hanging on the wall behind him. The squeaking of an expo marker steals the silence from the room.

"Good," coach says.

He talks to himself quite a bit, it freaks me out because I don't know if I should respond with anything. I remember the time during one of our games, he was so pissed at the referee, calling penalties left and right and out of the blind. He would violently yell his red tomato face off at the referee, but all of them would ignore his creative language. I don't blame them for doing so, it's not like that conversation would go anywhere. But that's when I kept my ears flush to his heated breath. If I were lucky to be sent onto the ice, and coach said my name, but I didn't realize it, he would announce his anger to the whole arena. Even the stereo system in the rink can't get that high in volume.

"Let's go win a game," he says.

Coach is about to leave but the door magically opens for him. Charlie and Jake walk in from behind the door with steaming cappuccinos in their hands.

"Boys," coach says.

"Coach," Jake says.

He leaves the room.

"We're warming up, Liam," Jake says.

"Oh," says I. "Okay."

I'm lucky Jake mentioned it to me, or else they probably would've forgotten about me. I muffle my ears with my headphones and resume my warmup playlist. Jake and Charlie lead the way out as I follow them to the bleachers. We jog up the steps to find the boys grouped up at the upper platform. A wooden trophy case displays old photographs and gold plastic trophies from Dorcha's teams. There were other legit trophies in the case that looked custom made of marble, but most of them were cheap knick-knacks from a thrift store.

Ben and Danny stand in front of our two lines. Ben always leads our warmups, and of course, Danny needs to be by his side at all times. I wonder if Ben gets annoyed with the constant weight on his back. It doesn't matter, those two have been holding hands ever since elementary school. Luckily, I didn't have to deal with them. My school was out in the countryside, named after a dinky stream, out in the woods. They had the privilege to attend the city school where all the popular kids came from.

Ben sprints down the hallway, Danny jogs his way down. Ash and Chester are the next two in line. They race each other in an aggressive sprint, their fists punching an invisible boxing bag in front of them and their feet hopping off the ground like the hallway is a pit of hot rocks. At the end of the hallway, they tie each other in the race, slamming into the wall. The wall is made of plank wood and contains a white door. Dorcha's locker room is unique as it sits on the second floor, inside a cubicle room that stands next to their fan section. I remember last year's game; they ran down a few spiral steps as the crowd hyped them up with energy.

Thomas and I are next in line. We push off the cold concrete and sprint down the hallway. I reach the end and feel completely breathful. It's a great sign that I'll have an awesome game today, or at least I'll be physically ready. Nothing's worse than feeling heavy on the ice with no adrenaline running through the veins. Those are the days when school drains all our energy, or coach burned our legs out the day before. Either way, it sucks that you can't do anything to change it. Staying hydrated helps but nothing really boosts your energy before the game. I've tried cappuccino, pre workout, but nothing seems to work these days.

Cole sprints down the hall by himself as Jake and Charlie goof their way down. Their always bubbly characters, I don't mind that they goof off and have fun, their just here to play hockey, but then there is Ben and Danny who do it for the attention. They want to be the biggest superstars in the state, but they don't put in enough work towards their goals. Nothing is going to be handed to you in life. You need to drain yourself out to the point of exhaustion to get anywhere. Danny needs to lose weight and stop drinking so much pop, and Ben needs to stop thinking about all the girls he could attract in his future and how huge of a superstar he'll be playing college hockey, but he honestly has no chance of going anywhere. He thinks he's an outstanding player, but he only scores most of his goals against the easy teams. These teams consist of a lack of motivation, poor defense, and awful goaltending, but I'm proud of the kids who don't exactly care about their overall record, they care about playing a game of hockey with one another, and that's really all that matters. Time will move on and then we'll all die in the end. I'd rather bring memories to Heaven with me than statistics.

Ben skips off with high knees, Danny follows but slows down halfway. How does coach see first line potential in that kid? This is ridiculous and embarrassing, he's the face of our first line. Chester should take his spot; he competes in cross-country in the fall for pete's sake. Chester and Ash skip their high knees down, Thomas and I follow. My legs are long, and my thighs are more built, I can't get my knees as high as I want them to, but I always accept the challenge to get my knees to my chest. High knees never seem to help my legs, but sometimes, you just have to go through the motions and wish for the best.

Once we all get back, the next exercise on the list is cherry pickers. Now, this is my kind of expertise. I'm the highest jumping player on this team. I love cherry pickers because they stretch out the legs but yet it boosts your energy up with a kick of adrenaline. As we leap our way across, our fingers tempt to touch the rafters along the ceiling. Give a bunch of kids a jungle gym and expect them to construct a few ideas.

We finish our group stretches with side lunges. Nothing beats the cracking of bones and the taffy pulls of the muscles. Legs is the most critical thing to stretch out. If your legs don't feel refreshed after stretching, then how do you expect to feed the wolf? That's why most of us do individual stretching. I walk over to the fence on the platform and throw a leg over it. I reach my arm to my foot and bend my body with the direction of my leg. I face towards the Dragon's section. Their heaters are blasting warmth as our section is dormant in the cold. The Dorcha kids pop out from behind their bulky locker room. They work out as a team under the scoreboard. Many of them wear headphones and have grins upon their attitude. Their team looks organized; straight lines, even lengths between them, almost as if they were training for the military.

I switch legs and face towards the front entrance as I reach for my other foot. Coach Kipp and the Dragon's coach talk to each other by the boards, a cup of coffee in their hands. Just the ordinary conversation of two coaches, secretly hating it but forcing their team's accomplishments into each other's throats.

Danny walks by the coaches, ditching personal stretches. Figures. Ben watches him leave to the locker room; he doesn't say anything but he's definitely thinking about something. Come on big guy, are you going to say anything to him? He must think he has a free ticket to leave since he's a first liner. How bout coach moves him down to second line, because some of us hate following a leader who doesn't have the credentials or the enthusiasm to put in some hard work. I'm shocked he's still eligible to play, his grades might be above average this year.

Wouldn't be surprised if his parents pay the school to keep his grades up. Their filthy loaded while his dad runs a restaurant business, explains a few things about his attitude and work ethic.

Ash and Chester finish their stretches and head down to the locker room. Cole is bouncing a ball off the wall near me. Thomas must be in the locker room already. Jake and Charlie follow the other guys down. It's almost game time. I walk down the bleachers to find the Dragon's coach looking at me. I act tall and modest, sneaking in a smile. His hairy racoon face smirks back.

THE STORM

The blare of the buzzer signals the end of warmups. Dorcha
outnumbers our student section by over half, but we had a decent
show up for tonight. We mostly have the clicky girls; they come to
support Ben, Danny, and Cole. Once in a while, Jake and Charlie
will get some girls supporting them, but I've never had that
experience. Ash, Chester, and I never had anyone in the stands
holding up signs with fancy slogans on them. We weren't as well
known, nor were we cool enough to be friends with the popular
kids. I'm totally fine with staying outside of the drama, but it
would be nice for someone to hold up a sign for me. I'm just that
typical popular-unpopular kid who's well known but doesn't have
too many close friends.

    The parents sit above the student sections. Our parents are a
smaller group as we are a smaller team. Dorcha packs into their
section like riding one of those New York City subways.
Everyone's crammed onto one another, making it harder for them

to leave their spots.

Our section is more spread out like stars twinkling in the night. They're scattered into their little groups. Two guys stand on the top platform; one leans against the fence in front of him, his arms crossed for support of his chubbier body, the other stands beside him with crossed arms over his chest. The chubbier one is Danny's spoiled father, and the one on the right is Ben's father. Their wives sit below them on the orange bleachers, chit-chatting. A few other parents and kids sit amongst the bleachers. They're all wrapped up in jackets and blankets with the heaters in our section turned off. Beanie hats bundle their heads in warmth, an unnecessary way of warmth.

My mom. She stands alone on the upper platform, all the way on the left side of the two dads. She watches us on the ice, finishing our warmups and preparing for battle. Ben and Danny's moms turn their heads to look at mom. They turn back to Dorcha's team with scrunching eyes of disgust. My mom keeps her quiet composure, staring at our team with a flat face.

I skate to the net to pick up pucks. One puck smacks the crossbar, sending a *ting* across the entire arena. Danny shoots a puck while I'm scooping them out of the net. Screw off, Danny, before the referees get a bad reputation of us. It's not just a pet peeve for the refs but one for me too. His shot isn't even that powerful. I would say his stick seems flimsy, but, in all honesty, his arms are the problem, floppy like the character balloons outside of car dealerships. Maybe he should hit up the gym once in a while, but he'd rather stay home and play video games all day.

I throw the pucks across the ice to the score box. A white bucket sits outside of the penalty doors where the referees stand. Some Dorcha players pick up the pucks while Chester and Thomas help out. Ben stands near the bench swigging water. The rest of the guys skate around till one of the refs blows his black plastic whistle. All the pucks are out of the net and we skate around our zone. We encircle Cole and his net like a shrinking merry-go-round. We yell out "Knights" as game time has finally reached.

Hardcore dubstep music vibrates the ground with screaming girls from Dorcha's section. The scoreboard sets for twenty minutes on the dot. Ben and Danny skate to center ice as I do the same. Jake and Charlie skate up from behind me, lining themselves up with the outside dots. I move over to the left hashmarks, bend my knees down, and watch as the referee is ready to drop the puck. Then I realize Dorcha's team is still doing their stupid chant at their net.

Dorcha players invade the bench as their first liners roll up to center ice. The left winger looks me down before getting into position. He's no taller than me, five foot ten. His mask is white, like Ben's and Danny's. Must be a first line thing, I've never cared for what color my mask is. Hockey is not about appearance, it's about playing the game and working as a team, but first liners will be third liners, and third liners will be underdogs. Coaches want their team to look like a strong army full of muscled men but looking the part doesn't mean receiving it. Put your third stringers out there and you'll be an undefeatable army.

The referee tweets his whistle and drops the puck. Ben battles for the puck with the centerman, but they pull the puck back. He hands it off to the right defenseman. I skate inside-out and target for him. I loop around to time my hit. He flutters the puck into our zone as I slam his forearms into the boards. His stick falls out from his hands.

The puck is in our defensive zone, sliding into the corner left of Cole's net. Jake competes the right winger in a sprinting race to the puck. They both slow up as Jake's body goes into the boards and the right winger sticks behind him. The puck is in front of his stick, but he's tied up. Dorcha's centerman picks up the puck and wraps around the net. Ben stands next to Cole, puppy guarding the goal line. Danny follows the puck carrier along the hash marks.

I cover the front of the net with Jake. Charlie pushes the centerman to the outside as Ben coasts from behind him. Danny moves over to his breakout spot on the far hash marks. The centerman throws his shoulder into Charlie. Danny pushes forward at the player. He throws the puck around Danny, bouncing off the boards to the high defenseman. The player passes the puck over to the defenseman for a one timer. He slams his stick on the ice. His stick physically bends into a bow, launching the puck at Cole. He deflects the puck with his left blocker, and the puck flies into the corner again.

Jake picks the puck up as the right winger runs in for a hit. I rush over to my hashmarks on the left dot. He passes the puck up to me just before he's slammed into the boards. I whip my head around in caution; this is the worst position to be in as a winger. When you're breaking the puck out, you need to have your head on a pivot at all times. Defenseman see bonus points when a winger receives a breakout pass, especially if their head is looking down at the puck. Luckily, the defensemen are backing out of the zone.

I shove my feet into the ice, accelerating with every push off the dull thin blades. The cool wind that swifts by dries my eyes into a cold desert. Mother says it's probably allergies, but it sucks because it makes me feel sleepy, but not tonight. I'm going to skate this puck pass this cocky defenseman (he's going to push me to the outside of the boards for a hit), but he doesn't know the speed that he's dealing with. I'm a rocket that NASA has secretly produced, turbo jet engines that can launch me into space within seconds. My feet will gallop around yours before you can even lay a finger on me.

I cross over the offensive blue line, and Ben skates around the other defenseman towards the net. I turn my turbo skates on and rush next to the defenseman, shoving my shoulder into his waist. Ben's stick reaches by the hashmarks. I throw the puck hard out in front of his momentum. He tips the puck as it misses the net and bounces into the far corner. Dorcha's centerman appears out of nowhere and turns the puck north.

I twist my body and sprint north, following the crowd. Their right winger slashes behind Charlie for a bump pass. The centerman holds the puck and skates to the center of the ice. He passes over to the left winger who has taken right winger's spot. They rush into the zone, three on two with Jake and Charlie skating backwards. Jake slows down as they enter the zone, I'm

sprinting back from behind. The player slows down in front of
Jake, moving towards the center of the ice. I skate into the zone
and bolt to my standing dot in the left circle. The right winger
looks to pass to his centerman and left winger, but Danny and
Charlie have them covered on the far side. He wrists a shot at
Cole, smacking him in the mask (a goalie's favorite) with a dead
clank. The puck flutters in the air and lands in the blue crease.
Cole falls down to his goalie position and finds the puck in front
of him. He covers the puck and tucks it into his leg pads.

The referee stops play with the tweet of his whistle. Cheers
and claps come from both student sections. Cole's mother cheers
him on as any goalie mom should do. She has that typical look for
a goalie mom: straight blonde hair that pulls down to the
shoulders, blue eyes outlined with mascara, and powdered-up
cheeks. I'm not big into makeup, but it's easy to tell when one has
it on. My mother could care less about makeup, and I support her
on that. She just throws on her glasses, curls her short, dirty
blonde hair, and calls it good.

She stands on the top platform with that same look on her
face. Those eyes just speak of something, focused and bold. She's
wanting me to do something that stands out. She wants me to
score a goal. I want to score goals to prove Coach Kipp wrong.
It'd be nice to rub it in with the first liner's parents here. They
think their kids are all stars, always at the bar on the weekends and
walking down the hallways thinking they own the place. The
moms would strut down the hallways like they are walking on the
red carpet, swinging the shoulders back and forth with their silver

purses slinged over them. The dads always stay away from their wives, acting so tough with bulked-out chests and pissed off faces; not once do they smile, unless they told a joke to one another, then they might sneak in a smirk and a chuckle.

I look at the scoreboard and discover the fact they we have been out here for roughly three minutes already. This beats my record for playing time in one shift throughout high school, besides that one time we were killing off a penalty kill with the Huskies last year, we could not throw that puck out of the zone.

Coach Kipp isn't pulling us out. I'm going to need a change, my breathing will turn into a pant, give it another shift or two. Some salty sweat drips off my nose and dissolves into my lips. Water sounds refreshing right now, I'd down it like Niagara Falls.

Dorcha changes lines. The referee tweets his whistle on the right-side faceoff dot. I position myself in front of the net with the opposing defenseman. The puck drops with Ben pulling it back for a faceoff win. Charlie receives it, skates it back into our defensive zone, and passes it behind the net to Jake. I backup to my boards for a breakout pass. Jake keeps the puck, but then passes it to Ben who loops around. Dorcha backs out of our zone, their centerman and left winger chasing us from behind. Ben passes the puck over to Danny who's open on the right side. The defenseman pressures Danny when he crosses the offensive blue line. Danny backhands the puck to Ben. Ben takes a shot at the net. The goalie deflects the puck with his leg pad, and it trickles into the far corner. Ben rushes to the puck. He bounces the puck off the boards to Danny who sits high in the zone. Danny takes the puck and walks the top of the circle. I move around the guarding defenseman with a huge slot opening for a backdoor shot. I raise my stick in the air and load up power in my legs. As I slowly drift to the goalie's backdoor, Danny sees my stick wide open. He holds the puck for another second before shooting a wimpy wrist shot at the goalie. Before I can pound the puck from under the goalie's glove, the referee tweets his whistle.

Danny! Why the fuck didn't you pass the puck?

Dorcha keeps their second line out. The scoreboard glows in thin neon lights, 14:57. My breath is caught in the fact that Danny didn't pass the puck. We could be up by one goal right now. I could have scored a goal. Everybody would be cheering, coach would be happy, mom would be proud of me, we'd be winning the game. Instead, Danny took one of the wimpiest wrist shots I've ever seen.

Danny hops onto the bench while his body burns the fat off. Coach Kipp sends Chester out to play right wing. He stands in front of me on the hashmarks in front of Dorcha's net, faceoff on the right circle. With another tweet of the whistle, the referee drops the puck. Ben loses the faceoff. Dorcha's defenseman steals the puck and sprints north with it. They approach our defensive zone with the puck. Charlie and Jake are the only ones who can stop them right now. Charlie cuts in and aims for a big collision with the puck carrier along our bench side, but he times it out too soon. The puck carrier dangles to the middle of the ice for a two-on-one with Jake.

I can hear coach's frustration as I chase from center ice.

Charlie's gonna get a yellin for that one. Defenseman need to time their hits out because if they go in too early, then the forwardman will simply make a move around the inside. Charlie knows he made a bad decision too; coach's yelling is just the cherry on top. Many cherries that is.

I'm backchecking from behind, Ben is somewhere behind me. The puck carrier passes the puck over to their right winger. He passes the puck right back to him as he one times the puck to the net. It flies right over the top of Cole's glove and bangs the glass.

The right winger skates to the puck, Charlie moves down low and shoves his body into the boards. The defenseman cross checks Charlie in the back, he falls down to the ground. I sprint over to the corner and pound the kid's head into the glass. A tweet of the whistle stops the clock, but it didn't stop the brawl of players in the corner. Fists are thrown everywhere; some wimps grab each other's jersey and pull each other down.

Charlie lies on the ground in the midst of all the blades. He tightens up into a ball to avoid getting stepped on. I throw a few more punches into this kid's gut while the others are surrounding me, keeping the refs out from our fight. I let the boy go and he steps back, wailing his arms in the air and stumbling to the ground.

Blood soaks through Charlie's jersey on his right arm. He holds it tight to himself, squeezing his eyes shut and holding in the pain. A couple of hands grasp my shoulders. They pull me back away from Charlie. The defenseman lies on the ground, throwing a kick to Charlie's head with his bloody blade.

The referee pulls me further away from him. Jake grabs the kid and pulls him away from Charlie. Cole helps and pushes the defenseman out of the area. The other referee sneaks into the little groups to break up their mini brawls.

Parents from the bleachers yell blasphemy and our student section bangs on the glass with their fists.

I'm thrown inside of the penalty box where an older man stands. He closes the door and locks it with the big metal lever. He walks to the side of me and pushes me away from the wall.

"Number 21," the old man says.

He walks back to the door, shoving the metal handle down and opening it for the medic. She's in her younger twenties, a skinny brunette in modern day leggings, and a white jacket speckled with black dots like poppyseeds on a muffin. She shimmies her feet on the ice over to Charlie, but he's up on his feet and skating to the bench already.

One of the refs skates over to the box.

"What's the call!" Coach Kipp says.

A five-minute penalty inputs to the scoreboard for the Knights.

"What!" coach says. "Where's their fucking behalf! Are you kidding me! That kid slammed my player from behind!"

The referee skates back to our defensive zone, but coach hops down from the bench and grabs his arm.

"Let go!" the ref says.

"Where's the fucking call!" coach says.

"Your guy threw a punch at him!"

93

"Because that fucking defenseman cross checked our guy! He skated up from behind him and jammed his stick to the back of his spine!"

"Calm down!"

"Don't tell me to calm down! Our player is bleeding out because of that kid! Did you not see the fucking hit!"

"I saw a clean hit from my angle."

"Geezes fucking Christ!"

Coach Kipp paces and wipes his face with his hand. Dorcha switches out their line back to the first liners. Charlie sits on the bench while the medic wraps his arm with gauze, thickening it to make his arm look like a marshmallow. Blood soaks through it, but it'll have to do for now.

"You need one more player, coach," the ref says.

Ben, Chester, and Jake stand at the right circle in our defensive zone.

"Ash," coach says. "Go out and kill." He looks over to Ben and waves him down.

Ben hops onto the bench.

"Coach," the ref says. "You still need a player."

"Give me a fucking second!" he says. Coach bends down to one knee over by Charlie. "Are you good to go?"

"I think so," Charlie says.

"He's going to need stitches," the medic says.

"He can get them after. We have a game to finish."

The medic unrolls Charlie's sleeve over the gauze, then walks off the bench. Charlie follows her off and onto the ice. She walks through the penalty box's door and the old man locks it shut.

Of course, no penalty is called for Dorcha. They hate us!
Even the refs despise our team, but maybe coach is to be blamed
for that. His attitude towards this team is like no other. They have
been defeating our team for years, and he dislikes the Dragons'
coach. I don't like either of them. All they want to be are powerful
dictators, but I don't understand. We're not even in the same
section! Their single A, and we're double AA.

If there's one thing that comes out positive about my
unfavorable penalty, it's that Ash and Chester can finally get some
playing time in.

The tweet of the whistle and the drop of the puck commences
the clock again.

The game's tough to watch through the obscured glass. Ben
and Danny are in the way. I stand up to watch the game, but the
old man tells me to sit down. I sit down, not wanting to start
another useless argument with these people. The Dragons have a
horrible community with disrespectful people, they can't even turn
the heaters on for our section. I can see the cold breaths from a
few children across the ice, shivering next to their mothers.

Two guys stick out from the ordinary on our bleachers. I've
never seen them at our games before. They wear formal winter
jackets, greased up hair that flows to the side of their head, and
they have wooden clipboards in their hands. A couple of guys in
formal clothes with clipboards at a hockey game can only mean
one thing. They're scouts.

Finally, maybe they'll recognize my playing efforts. Yes, I

got a penalty, but that shows my strength and how I'm protecting my teammates. Everything before the penalty, I was in my correct positions, open for goal opportunities, but if only Danny would have passed the puck. I hope the scouts aren't just here for Dorcha. I wonder what their opinion on the penalty would be.

The Dorcha crowd bursts into screaming fireworks. The Dragons score a goal. My penalty has four more minutes. This is going to be a long hockey game.

Up on the platform where my mom stands, Ben's dad clenches his face while looking at the players. On his right, Danny's dad leans over the rail and turns his face at mom.

"Great," Ben's mom says. "Now we're going to lose against Dorcha."

"Well," Danny's mom says. "If it wasn't for Liam's penalty."

"Hey," mom says. "If you're going to talk tough like that, then say it to my face next time."

"Maybe I will," Danny's mom says.

"And tell your son to pass the puck once in a while."

"What a fucking bitch," Ben's mom says.

"What did you just say, Chloe?"

Aw! Yes! That's her name. I remember now. Chloe is Ben's mother, and I can definitely tell that's her from all the way over here in the box. She has that attitude of a white girl; coffee in hand, black leggings, white furry jacket, and again, a fully loaded powdered face. Danny's mother, I forgot her name. What is it again?

"She said you were a fucking bitch," Danny's mom says.

"I asked her, Lexi," mom says.

Oh! Lexi is Danny's mother. I can read my mom's lips. Must be some heavy drama over there if I can read em from here.

Danny's dad walks around Ben's father and points at the door near my mom. They seem to be arguing. My mother walks away and down the steps. Her hand wipes a few tears from under her glasses. She walks out the front doors into the darkness. This isn't the first time she's left a game early.

A roar of energy sprouts from Dorcha. They zip by their bench for their two-point lead. Coach whips a water bottle at the glass, startling me from my seat. Water explodes on the window, some of it spraying into the air and sprinkling onto my helmet.

The scoreboard displays my penalty to be another minute and forty-nine seconds. Dorcha switches back to their second liners. Chester and Ash lean their sticks on their knees, catching their breath. A tweet of the whistle and they're off to battle again. The Dragons win the puck back and play it slow while transitioning into our zone again.

Dorcha's advantage stresses me out to watch, but the old man stands up and sets his hand on the lever. I stand up in the box, ready to skate out and compete. Ten seconds before I'm out, and a Dorcha defenseman has the puck. He takes a hard slapshot. Ash deflects the puck with his shin pad. The puck pops out near Chester.

The old man lifts the lever up and pulls the door open. Chester flips the puck over the defenseman, flying high by the brown rafters on the ceiling, and then falling down on the far blue line. I sprint over to the puck for a break away opportunity. I take a hard snapshot as the puck flies for top shelf, but the puck *tings* off the crossbar and to the side of the net. The defenseman skates back and charges at me, but I blindly throw the puck backdoor just to find Ash shoving it into the net. Our student section screams in joy as we clash Ash in hugs against the boards.

We're down by one. Ash and Chester head over to the bench for a change. Ben and Danny lift their legs over the boards.

"No," coach says. "Ash, Chester, stay out there!"

Ash and Chester skate back out to center ice.

"A two-minute shift," coach says. "Then get off."

Ash takes center. Dorcha has their first liners out. With a tweet of the whistle, the ref drops the puck. Ash wins the faceoff, kicking the puck out to me. The right winger rushes to me, but I pass the puck back to Jake. He passes the puck along the blue line to Charlie. Charlie skates over the center red line and throws the puck deep into the offensive zone. It whirls around the edge of the boards to my side of the ice. I push off the ice and reach the puck near the goal line in the offensive zone. My momentum moves me behind the net. Chester comes at me from the other direction. We pass each other in the corner, swapping the puck to his stick. The defenseman stops and turns while Chester skates towards the net. I loop around the top of the circle, Ash moves backdoor. Chester finds an open slot to my stick. I pound the puck right over the goalie's leg pad. My arms launch into the air with the guys slamming into me with hugs. Our section cheers louder than the last. The adrenaline is really kicking in at this point, but I also feel short of breath after that run.

"Coach," says I. "I need a breather."

"Ben," coach says. "Go out for Liam."

Ben skates out to left wing.

"Nice goal," coach says.

I sit there panting as the water bottles taunt me with my exhaustion. It's never the best feeling to drink water while gasping for oxygen at the same time. It's like patting your head and rubbing your stomach, it's possible, but it takes practice. Besides, I feel hydrated enough to finish the game.

I look over to my right to find Danny looking at me with his stupid mouth wide open. Sometimes I catch him with his jaw dropped like he's in a frozen yawn or something. It's like he wants to say something dumb to me, but he never does. He looks away about three seconds after our mini staring contest.

I make eye contact with one of the kids sitting by the coach's feet on the Dorcha bench. It's the shaggy hair kid, the same one I saw walking into the arena on the bus. He's soaking in tears, sitting all alone on the bench. He looks at me with his hopeless stare, I can't even bother to look away. His tears soak into my eyes. They drip down the sides of my cheek, and then down my neck. I don't know why I'm crying. I don't know why he's crying. A headache expands its roots inside of my brain, the same type of headache when you lack sleep.

Screams from the Dorcha section ignites inside the arena.

We break eye contact. Dorcha scores another goal.

SHOCKER

The time flies by like a bald eagle as I find myself shaking hands
with the Dragons. We end in a lost against Dorcha, 2-5. No more
goals were scored for our team, but our energy stayed consistent
for the rest of the game, most of us at least. That one boy crying
on Dorcha's team keeps popping up inside of my thoughts. It
concerns me, this kid was staring into my soul. It's like he wanted
me to do something or say something. Maybe it has something to
do with his personal life; could be a girlfriend, his parents, his
puppy got ran over by a car. Something was upsetting him, and it's
taking a toll on me too. There was a powerful sense in him, like he
had some sort of superpower where he could speak to me with
utter silence. I can't explain what it was, but something was
connecting us.

As I pass the one crying boy in line, his eyes look straight
into the back of his teammate's head. We touch hands, then
butterflies ignite inside of me. Towards the end of the line, I shake

hands with the small Dorcha coach, then I head for the door. I follow Danny and Chester off the ice, stepping over the ledge to a rubber padding that trails along the floors. The ceiling closes in, feeling a lot tighter this time. A lightheadedness floats inside of my head while the ceiling pushes down on me with its invisible pressure. Being inside of an open arena and entering into a tight vault is not a pleasant transition. The lights are also dimmer, making my eyes want to sink.

We walk inside the locker room, bags all shoved under the benches. It's nice to have a little room to waddle in this little alleyway. Chester beats me to the corner bench as I sit down next to him. I unbuckle my helmet and toss it into my bag. Chester has ripped through his upper pads already, moving down to untie his skates. Honestly, he might be quicker at untying his skates than his sprinting records.

The rest of the guys come through the door, most with settled faces. Charlie giggles from something Jake says walking in; it kind of settles my brain down from the lightheadedness. Ben looks a little bored while holding his face down to the floor. We lost a game, but it's not one of those games to be upset about. As much as we dislike the Dragons, we played a great game tonight. I'm guessing he's upset about his playing time. He didn't score any goals and didn't get any assists, but you're not always going to be a stellar player. Even the best of the best have down days, you just have to learn how to climb out of that dark chamber like the rest of us.

Ash squats down beside me. "Dude! Did you see me lay out

that kid?"

"In the third?" says I.

"Yeah! I rammed his head so hard into the glass."

"That was awesome!"

"I'm not gonna lie, but I probably should've had a boarding call for that."

"Nah, Dorcha deserved it."

"That's a little harsh," Chester says.

"Nah, did you see what they did with the heaters?" says I.

"No?"

"They only turned the heaters on for their section! They never turned our heaters on."

"Really?" Ash says.

"Yeah," says I.

"Nice job tonight, boys!" Chester says.

"Dude, that was so fun!" Ash says. "Those kids were chirping the hell out of us."

"Yeah, and one kid kept slashing me with his stick," Chester says.

"Oh my God, was it the one who'd always tap your shin on a faceoff?"

"Yes! He was driving me nuts!"

"Did you whack him back?" says I.

"No," Chester says. "I wish, but then the stupid ref would give me a stupid penalty."

"Yeah," Ash says. "Home ice advantage is a bitch."

"When is our next home game?" says I.

"Not sure," Chester says.

"Dude," Ash says. "What day is it today?"

"Tuesday," Chester says.

"I don't know why. I just completely forgot!"

"Yep, school tomorrow."

I'm glad to see Ash so joyful after the game. He's never this happy after hockey games, and I can understand where he's coming from. The thought of having school tomorrow tires me even more, until something flickers my eyes into an awakening.

"WOOOOOOOOO!" Charlie announces. "No school tomorrow, baby!"

We all get up from our benches and celebrate. Jake gives Charlie a chest bump and they do some cool handshake. Danny tunes on some awful rap music into the boombox, but who cares, we have no school tomorrow. Thomas and Cole sit comfortably with their bulky leg pads still strapped on. Ben watches Jake and Charlie get into a silly dancing groove. I have no clue what I'm watching but it's very entertaining. It has a mix of rodeo kicks and spins, a dance you usually find with some sort of Irish music; blaring bagpipes, a kicking bass drum, electric guitar strumming in the background, it's perfect to lighten up the atmosphere in the locker room.

Coach Kipp walks into the locker room but stops with the sight of Jake and Charlie busting out their moves. He smirks and nods his head in agreement. Man, why does he always have to make things so awkward? Probably because he's in his late forties, and his hair is short, and his face is always burning red, and he's our coach, and I can see him as a pedophile, and that's a weird thought I'm gonna slide under the bench.

Charlie notices Coach Kipp in amusement. He points at coach and laughs his head off. Jake takes a seat with blush upon his face. I can't hear the laughter over the rap music, but the chitter-chatter gets louder when Ben turns the volume all the way down.

"I see Charlie and Jake are trying out for the dance team," coach says.

"They're just excited we have no school tomorrow!" Thomas says.

"What's that?"

"We have no school tomorrow," Charlie says.

"They called it off?" coach says.

"Yeah!"

"Sweet. That means I get to sleep in."

Coach Kipp expects a laugh after his cringey jokes, but we all just end up smiling at him, and it gets quite awkward. Once his voice is the only one talking in the room, that's when it's really awkward. I can never imagine having a normal conversation with him. Must be his age that makes it weird to think about.

"Alright," coach says. "Good game tonight, boys! We lost this game by what, like two goals or something. Not a big deal! I actually think that's the best we've played all year. Dorcha is a tough team; they have two D-commits. Not an easy team, but you guys worked hard and didn't stop competing. So, let's pack up our things and hop on the bus."

Some of the boys continue to cheer after coach finishes his

talk. He walks over to Ben and says something to him. Ben stands up from the bench and walks out with coach. I can only think of what bad things are going to happen out there. After what Finn told me on the bus ride home that one night . . . I can't even think about it. The scars, the bruises, the tears that flowed streams down his soft cheeks, even the tight brotherly squeeze he gave me, I can just feel him hugging me right now.

Ash rips the velcro straps on his elbow pads, taking me out of the thoughts about Finn. I too take my gear off, starting with my jersey and working my way down to my skates. Chester has all of his clothes on, and he walks out of the locker room with his hockey bag. The bus isn't going to leave for another ten minutes cause Ben never took his gear off, and now he's getting the talk with coach.

"Hey," Ash says. "Do you and Chester want to go to Carbone's tonight?"

"Well," says I. "It'll be midnight by the time we get back."

"They always stay open till three."

"I guess."

"Plus, I'm fucking starving!"

"True, you got me there!"

"I can just feast right now!"

The door props open as Ben walks back in. Coach must have just talked with him about something. No bruises, no scars, no slashes, nothing. I think I even see some happiness in him, but it's hard to tell with his always-so-serious looking face.

"What was that about," Danny says.

"Two guys talked to me about practicing with their team next week," Ben says.

The scouts. The two men in the bleachers sitting below the conversation my mom was in with Chloe and Lexi, they had the clipboards in their hands, they were scouts. My assumptions were leaning towards scouts, but I am shocked to see they asked a player from our team, especially Ben. He didn't even have a good game tonight. Oh my God! I just had one of the best games of my life. Me, Chester, and Ash rocked out there on the ice. We were the only ones who made productive plays out there, the only ones who scored our two goals. Why in the world would they ask Ben?

It didn't take me long to realize why they probably asked Ben. I bet my life away that they were only looking at the stats on the fucking clipboards and didn't even bother to watch the game. When they were watching, they only had the few numbers in mind that were circled on their sheet. I wonder if they even cared that our line scored goals tonight. But just like most modern politicians, business owners, and social media addicts, they only care about the numbers. Scouts don't look for the hard-working players who work out at the gym every day, skate on a sheet of ice every night, pressure themselves to be better constantly, physically checking players to their knees, none of that matters to them. They only want the players who can score goals for their teams, the playmakers. But that doesn't make any sense because these guys didn't make any fucking plays tonight. It was our line who did fricken amazing out there! We put on a great show for our audience tonight. Are they blind? Did they not realize how great of a candidate me or Chester or Ash can be to their team? Man, all these scouts, all these upper-class teams in the higher leagues, they're just pure greed. It seems like they all forget what makes a team a true team. You can't just load a team with a bunch of goal scorers, you'd just make a team filled with greedy puck hogs, or at least you'd be adding one to your team. Why not aim for the players who work their asses off every day to the point of depression? That's gold ice right there! There's so much potential in the players who actually want to do this sport as a living, but scouts find a way to fuck it up. Greed, that's what their made of, and greed is what kills the opportunity for a great hockey team. Why ask a rich man for help when you know he's not going to? Ask the poorer ones to help you, they're the ones who will put in the hard-fucking labor to help you succeed in the end. And most teams are running under a dictatorship. These days, it's hard to tell if we're the ones playing the hockey game or if the coaches are. It just feels like we're a bunch of pawns being played upon a chess board.

Finally, I unlace my skates, slide my bottoms off, throw on some clothes, and walk out of the locker room with my bag. At the end of the claustrophobic hallway, some Dorcha parents stand in little groups. Some of the parents glance at me, but nothing too concerning. I pass by and exit through the front doors, which weren't really front doors since they were located on the side of the building, but they were the main doors to get inside the arena.

The snow outside is half a foot deep. The sidewalks aren't cleared yet, so I trudge my way through the thick fluff to the trailer. I throw my bag in, not caring where it lands at this point. If it's in the way of anything, someone else can move it. The fluffy snow sticks to the top of my curls and cools my head off as I hop onto the bus.

I can't wait to eat pizza, but this'll be an interesting ride home.

SALT AND PEPPER

The darkness from outside creeps through the frosted windows.
The headlights of the bus shine on the giant parmesan flakes
falling from above. Snow blankets the road in a heaping one foot.
We're traveling on highway 21 about half under the speed limit,
thirty miles per hour or so. The Barn is only a few minutes away,
but it'll take longer at this rate. As long as our bus driver gets us to
our destination in one piece, I'll be thankful. It's like a customer
leaving the donut store with a box of donuts. You don't want to
move the box around too much, or else the frosting will smear the
cardboard it's riding in, and donuts aren't as sweet without the
frosting. So, take it slow on the roads, handle us with care like
we're your donuts in a cardboard box.

I choose one of the best seats to lounge in. The heater is
placed right below where my feet rest. The thick warmth heats up
my sweatpants, bundling me in my own cozy cocoon. It gives me
that type of feeling of being crowded by a bunch of people, not

like jam packed inside of a concert, but centered in the middle of everything. It's like nothing can hurt me or the others sitting around me, but if anything happens to anyone, it would be the ones sitting on the outside. Having more boys on the team to fill these bus seats would add to the coziness, but our team is so small.

This is the one reason why we shouldn't be competing in double AA hockey, but apparently a stupid school population modifies everything for sports. The Huskies are single A because of their school size, but their hockey team is made up of gigantic beasts. They have four lines with some guys ranging up to six and a half feet. It would make more sense to move them up to double AA since they go to state every year, but it doesn't seem like they're up for that challenge.

Chester lays his body across the seat on the other side of the bus, his feet resting on mine. Ash is behind him, looking at something on his phone with the blinding white light shining upon his face. Charlie's head lazes on Jake's shoulder towards the back of the bus. Ben and Danny obtained their cool back-of-the-bus seats like always. Cole and Thomas sit somewhere in the back, but Cole is probably on his phone, and Thomas can be listening to music while slouching in his seat. Coach Kipp is in his front seat by the bus doors.

The bus turns left off of Highway 21. A few bumps over the train tracks indicates that we're home. As I look for The Barn in front of the bus, I notice a boy standing in the middle of the road. The streetlight on the left side of the road illuminates his body through the falling fluff. Coach Kipp stares out the front window.

The bus driver continues driving, not showing any signs of slowing down. Does he not see the kid? He is an older fella, but the boy is clearly there, not even the falling flakes can disturb his silhouette.

We approach closer and closer to the boy. I look around to see if anyone else is seeing this. Chester grabs his jersey off the window. Ash still looks at his phone. The guys in the back seem to be rummaging for their things. They're always in a rush to get off the bus, and sometimes they'll try to beat me to the front of the bus, but if it's really that important to be the first one off, then sit in the front.

The kid stands still, and the bus is still moving at its steady twenty mile per hour rate. No one is saying anything, and the bus driver is clueless. What do I do? Maybe I should yell at him. I don't know whether to believe my eyes or not. It can just be a shadow of something from inside the light. It can be some sort of scientific phenomenon when light bends shadows into different shapes or something. It can be a snowman a child built in the middle of the road that the bus driver wants to plow through. But whatever it is, I'm about to see it get ran over by our school bus. The bus inches closer and closer, creeping onto the kid.

Before I can release anything into words, I duck into my seat and cover my ears with my hands. I squeeze my head as if it were a zit, squeezing and squeezing until it would burst into gush. My heart pumps the blood through my veins like it's a machine that's out of control and ready to explode. The blood crawls through my veins like a trail of ants. They crawl through my whole body, making every inch itch in desperation for a scratch, but my hands are glued to my head.

A sudden double tap on my shoulder startles me. I release my hands and dart my eyes over to find Jake in the aisle of the bus.

"Hey," Jake says. "Are you okay?"

"Ugh, yeah."

"Are you sure, dude?"

"Yeah. I'm fine. You just startled me."

"Sorry."

"Don't be! I was just having a bad dream."

But was it a dream? No. I know I was awake, but what happened to those sudden seconds on the road? They just vanished like I was drugged up on lidocaine. I've always heard people talk about falling asleep for their wisdom teeth removal, and it's just bizarre to hear all of them say it's sorta like a nap. I don't know what being drugged up is like, and I'd like to keep it that way, but I bet this is what it feels like. You just suddenly wake up from a deep sleep and don't remember anything that happened. It's creepy to think that time can be taken out from our lives while our heart still beats. But I wasn't asleep, I was conscious!

Before I draw any more attention, I hop off the school bus and grab my gear from the trailer. I stomp the sticky snow off my shoes walking through the double set of french doors to The Barn. The rink is pitch black, but a few lights shine our way to the long hallway. I walk into the locker room and quickly hang up my gear to dry. I check my phone to notice it's almost one in the morning.

"I'll see ya guys at Carbones," Chester says.

"Get us a booth," Ash says.

I can taste the melting cheese on my tongue already. They seduced me into wanting pizza at this time of night, or morning. The thought of the burning tomato sauce, stretchy mozzarella cheese, pepperoni slices, all on top of a soft, doughy crust, sounds like Heaven. And why not celebrate the snow day we have tomorrow, or today, with the best pizza in town.

"Oh my God," Ash says. "I need to feast!"

"Yeah," says I. "I need to feast too!"

"I'll meet ya there!"

"Okay."

Ash beats me out of the locker room before I can even shove my bag in the cubby. Once I did, I go out into the long hallway and leave The Barn. Outside, the snow packs the ground with more fluff. My car is across the road that boy stood on. We always park our cars in the high school parking lot across the street. We don't choose to, we're forced to.

As I walk across the quiet street, I stop in my tracks and look for the kid. Gone. Gone like a whisper in the wind. The snow acts like sound proofers, deathening every little sound around it. I waddle my feet through the snow on the road and reach the curb. A snowbank, towering about twelve feet, obstructs the way to the parking lot. I walk around the snowbank to the parking lot's entrance and find my car layered in snow. When I open the door, shards of ice crackle off and dive deep into the snow.

I lunge myself into the driver's seat and turn on the car. The heaters blast cold air from the vents. There's no way I'm waiting for this car to heat up, but I need to clean off the windows. One of Minnesotans favorite sports to play in the winter that's not hockey: scraping. I scrape as fast as I can as the cold air dulges itself into my bare skin. The snow is easy to brush off, but very annoying as it flutters into my jacket and down my shirt. However, the ice is coarse like sandpaper. Wedging the scraper under the ice is tedious, but once I get it, the rest is a piece of cake.

I get back inside the car and pull out of the parking lot. The snow from under the tire flattens with its squeakiness of a leather jacket. Danny and Thomas come running around the snowbank. A snowball whips from around the corner. Jake chases them down to their cars. I drive out of the parking lot with caution to anymore silly animals running across the road.

As I drive down the road, I power on my radio for some sound. Never drive alone in silence.

"Pretty crazy out there, Kelly!" a man says.

"It is, Arnold!" Kelly says. "The storm has arrived, and it is furious! We've had some shocking reports recently from the St. Cloud area that thunderstorms have developed with this strong surge of moisture. Earlier, we also received a lot of photos of the wall cloud that pushed through the west and south metro with this system. Powers have been cutting out throughout the state, many across the city here in Minneapolis. Snowplows have been preparing days before the storm hit, packing up on salt and sand, and planning their routes. But nothing will keep these roads clean as the storm will last into tomorrow and early into Thursday morning. Back to you, Arnold."

"Thank you, Kelly," Arnold says. "Now, let's check in with meteorologist Mike Alignot from the weather center. Mike."

"Thank you, Arnold," Mike says. "Over a foot of snow has fallen over the last several hours and it will continue to pack up through the next upcoming days. The snow is not going to slow down anytime soon as this huge band of moisture stalls over us for quite some time. It'll eventually be pushed out by a cold front coming in from Canada and will head for Wisconsin. The storm should be gone by late Friday morning, but then a bitter blast of cold air will strike the state, taking temperatures from the teens and plummeting down to the negatives. Our systems predict the temperature to be sly of negative thirty degrees fahrenheit on Friday morning. If you are having to drive to work or have any plans for the weekend, I would plan to keep your vehicles in your garage as they will freeze up in this Arctic air. Back to you, Arnold."

Right as I pull into Carbones' parking lot, which is about half full, my heat finally decides to kick in. The heat inside the restaurant will comfort me more though. Hopefully, Chester has ordered the pizza for us already.

I hop out of the car and lock the door with my keypad. When I enter the front doors of the restaurant, I stomp my feet onto the slushed-up carpet, removing the snow from my shoes. No server stands at the podium. I peek around the right corner. Two tables are full of younger adults drinking alcohol and eating pizza. They look to be recent college graduates. A woman and a man are together in a booth, they have two glasses of wine and a plate of cheese cubes on their table. I can see Ash and Chester one booth down from the couple's booth.

"Aye yo," says I.

"I got you root beer," Chester says.

"Perfect!"

"How was your drive?" Ash says.

"Fine. Kinda scary though. I slid in a few spots, and I was only going twenty."

"Yeah! I was driving twenty-five, and I went around the bend, up by that small church, and my car started to drift on the other side of the road. I actually nicked the curb while a car was coming towards me. But I was lucky they turned into the suburbs."

"Yeah," Chester says. "Not gonna lie, that bus ride was kind of sketchy."

"Tell me about it!" says I. I take a few gulps of my root beer. "So, what do you guys think about with the whole Ben thing?

"About the scouts?"

"Yeah."

"It's fucking stupid," Ash says. "He's not even good!"

"I know, right! If only coach played us more, we'd have more goals on our record! Have you guys ever realized that we've never played a power play in high school yet?"

"Yeah," Chester says.

"Well, you might actually play next year, Chester," says I. "You still have some time. But once Ash and I graduate high school here--" Ash snorts. "We will graduate!"

"I'm just kidding," Ash says.

"Chester. Once we're gone, you'll be with the new wave of younger bantam kids. There's quite a bit of them actually, enough for three full lines I believe."

"Geezes," Chester says.

"Yeah," says I. "But for a few years now, Ash and I haven't played one single second of a power play. It's always been Ben, Danny, and--" Before I finish my line, I pause and look down to the floor.

"Coach is such a dumbass," Ash says.

"You got that right," Chester says.

"Watch him sit us the next game."

"He probably will."

"Do you guys think he was mad at me?" says I.

"For what?" Chester says.

"My penalty. Was he pissed at me?"

"He was pissed at the refs," Ash says.

"He didn't seem mad at you," Chester says. "He kept playing you."

"He's only playing me because I'm the only left winger on the team," says I.

"But you deserve it."

"It just feels like I'm being used. He's only using me because he needs someone to fill the spot."

"You're fucking strong, dude! And you're the fastest one on the team!"

"Thanks."

"Coach may not realize it, but we do. My mom always says

we need you."

"Really?"

"Yeah! My mom, Jake's mom, Thomas' mom, they think you and I should be playing first line all the time."

That made my night. I never knew anyone cared that much about me, or at least agreed on the same thoughts of mine.

A waiter walks over with a gigantic pepperoni pizza cut into little squares and sets it on the table. He places a pile of plates right next to it. Chester and Ash grab a plate, I grab the bottom one. I pull a few cheesy slices from the pan, having to rip a few strands with my bare fingers. The grease burns but it somewhat feels pleasing. Could be the fact that there's a storm outside, bringing the stale cold with it. But there's something else that feels cold.

Ash is quiet, almost too quiet.

WEALTHY WINES

A black BMW shines its white fluorescent lights up the snow-coated driveway. The tires track through the fluff, but the snowstorm will cover up the breadcrumbs in no time. Once the car stops and thrusts back into park, the fluorescent lights turn off. The rustic lights hanging between the three garage doors reflect warmth on the car's spotless exterior. Snow coats the car's hood while it sits there in silence.

It's a silent storm, indeed it is. A storm that will produce a beautiful aftermath. Then the children can play in the snow and wreck its smooth topping, just like the surface of ice cream in a gallon bucket getting its first scooping.

The house is huge, not enough to call a mansion, but definitely holds a bigger family inside. It appears like a modern Victorian, triangular points on the roof, a large porch with beams made of rocks and wood, white trimming surrounding the light grey siding, and large rectangular windows. Above the third stall on the left side, the outlier stall, parches out a small section from the roof. It has a tall, skinny rectangular window. To the right, above the other two stalls, parches out another window. From the outside, it looks to be the master bedroom and bathroom. The house angles to the right from the garage stalls. A maple door stands tall in the center of two rooms with giant windows, customized with white trimming. Three more custom windows are above the maple door. From behind the house, winter branches poke out in the town-lit night, like thorns on a bush, although, they are quite obstructed with all the falling snow. One pine tree towers by the outlier stall with its snowy ferns.

The driver door of the BMW opens. A black tennis shoe swings out and dangles above the snow that sheets the driveway, then the other shoe swings out. They plot down in the snow as a hand grabs the roof of the car. The hand pulls the body out that sits inside. It's Ben. He's dressed in his team's away outfit; black sweatpants with his maroon number 5 embroidered onto it, the team's sweatshirt which mocks the design of our home jersey with colors of a vibrant maroon, white, and black, and the beanie with our logo on it.

Ben tippy toes through the snow to the tall maple door. He stomps the snow off his black tennis shoes and heads inside the house. As he walks inside, he can tell the fireplace is lit. The coziness cuddles around him like an invisible blanket wrapping him up in a wolf's pelt. It's dark in the front entrance, the office on the right is pitch black, and so is the foyer on his left. The zig-zag stairs beside the office leads into a blackness; the basement one is the creepiest of them all. Ben never wants to know the monsters lurking behind that one corner of the zig-zag stairs.

Ben hears some chatter from the main floor. An older girl's voice casts through to him. He pulls off his shoes from his damp feet, then he walks towards the living room along the maple wood floors. The entryway into the living room is like the shape of an arched portico. There's an arched hole in the wall beside the portico entryway and the zig-zag stairs leading to the basement. A red flower vase with cherry blossoms rests inside of it.

The lights from the kitchen and dining room glow into the living room. Ben turns the corner to the sound of the voice. His older sister, Bethany, his older brother, Cambridge, and his parents sit around the dining table. The dark walnut table has a European design to it, almost as if the design mimicked a cathedral. Its design looks like a flower mixed with a seashell, but then around the figure resembles something like ocean waves in a midst of a whirlwind storm. The same flower looking design is on the tips of the leather chairs.

"That's awesome, sweetheart," Chloe says.

Bethany looks over from her mother to find Ben walking over to the table. Chloe pivots her head to him.

"Hey, Ben," Chloe says.

"Hey," he says. He stands behind the vacant chair right next to his mom.

"Bethany is back from school. She received an internship to Europe this summer."

"Nice."

Chloe reaches her hand over the walnut table to grasp a thin pedestal of a wine glass. "That's why we need to get you into Harvard. Maybe your father can help you out with that." She raises her eyebrows at Ben's father while she takes a sip of her bloody wine.

"I could probably have a talk with them," he says. "I'm sure we could come up with some sort of deal. But it would be much simpler if you could earn a perfect score on the ACT. Maybe I should schedule another testing for you, Ben. You still have a few more attempts available."

"I thought I already talked to you guys about this. I don't want to go to that school."

"Well, I think you just need more time to think," Chloe says. "Look how successful Bethany is doing. She's got a scholarship to Europe; she's already getting job offers her junior year."

"Good for her," Ben says. "But I don't like that school, mom. Besides, it's not like I'm going to make the hockey team for Harvard anyways."

"Your father could probably do something about that too, but you won't make any team with the way you played tonight." She takes another sip of her bloody wine.

"Really?" Cambridge says. "How was the game?"

"Awful," Chloe says. "Very embarrassing. Ben barely got to play. Coach Kipp kept putting out second line. Liam is also playing for both lines now and it sucks. He's definitely not first line potential."

Cambridge looks over to Ben. "Sounds like you guys need

more soldiers on the team."

"And tonight," Chloe says. "Tonight was the worst. Liam's mom, have you seen her?"

"The one that always wears those reading glasses that you say makes her look bitchy?"

"Yes! That's his mom, and she was being a bitch to me today."

"How so?"

Ben's interest spikes with this family conversation.

"She bitched at Lexi and I about Ben and Danny and told us how awful they are at hockey. She said you guys are puck hogs."

"I think she's jealous that you and daddy have money," Bethany says.

"Yes," Chloe says. "She is." She turns her body towards Ben. "Ben, you need to stand out on the ice. I don't want to see another embarrassing game."

"Your mother's right," his father says. "It's just like running a successful business, son. You need to sell yourself out there. You need to stick out from the competition. You need a scout to pull ya out to a team."

"Actually," Ben says. "I was asked by a scout tonight to practice with them."

"What!" Chloe says.

"Yeah. A scout asked for me after the game."

"That's great, son!" his father says.

"It's about time they asked," Chloe says. "I knew you were going to be asked sooner or later. It's just a matter of time." She gulps down the rest of her bloody wine. "So, when's the first practice?"

"Tomorrow," Ben says.

"Don't you have school tomorrow?"

"School's cancelled."

"Oh. And practice?"

"Coach made it sound like we won't have practice, but it'll probably still be on tomorrow, even with the storm."

"Well, make sure you let him know that you'll be missing then."

"I will."

"And go shower. You smell like wet dog."

FLIPPERS

Danny pulls off to the side of Main Street and parks his dinky silver car. No vehicles are present on Main Street. The town has an old western look to it, ones that you'd discover in the deserted plains. Main Street used to be a dirt road that horses would travel on. The concrete sidewalks were once wooden boardwalks that would erode in the snow and dust, but the historic buildings have stayed the same ever since. The old movie theater converted into a dance studio, the bank is a post office, and The Hotel Broz is a historical hotel right across from Flippers, the restaurant and bar that Danny's father owns.

Danny props the door open and hops out. He's still wearing the warmup clothes from hockey. As he turns around and shuts the car door, it slams on his right hand, crushing his fingers. He groans inside, hiding the pain from the possible spirits peeking through the hotel's windows. The car door is locked shut. He ravages in his fuzzy pockets and pulls out his car keys, which is connected to his school lanyard. He attempts to poke the key into the lock, but it falls into the snow. The snow burns his hand as he reaches into the fluff. He takes the key again and inserts it into the lock. He opens the door and releases his hands as the car echoes its blaring honk on Main Street. Danny powers the ignition on and back off. The horn stops. His fingers aren't bleeding, but he knows there'll be some nice bruises in the morning. Danny slams the door shut and heads inside.

The windows are blocked by the glowing neon signs that face out to Main Street. The lights inside are dim, and the televisions aren't on. Lexi sits at the bar with a beer bottle in front of her, his father is behind the bar. Creaks from the old wooden floors and squeaks from the front door bring their attention to Danny.

"Hey!" Lexi says. "What's up my dude?"

"Your grilled cheese is almost done," his father says.

"Good," Danny says. "I'm starving! I barely ate anything today."

"So, no school tomorrow, huh?" Lexi says.

"Yep," Danny says. "Thank God!"

Lexi takes a chug from her beer. "Didn't get much playing time today, did ya?"

"Well, I mean it was less than we usually get, but I was fine with it. I got to catch my breath before some of the shifts."

"Yeah. Second line was great today!"

"They put two goals up on that scoreboard," his father says.

"Chloe wasn't very pleased with that," Lexi says.

"Wait, why?" Danny says.

"She thought you and Ben didn't get the right amount of playing time for the night."

"I thought it was fine, just wish Liam would set me up for more scoring opportunities."

"Yeah. He doesn't have the chemistry that you and Ben always had. I was offended by the comment Liam's mom made about you."

"What did she say?"

"She said you were," Lexi needs to find an unharmful way to phrase this, "Slow."

"Well, I'm not the fastest on the team, but I'm not slow."

"I don't know who gave her the rights to say that, but I was supporting Chloe in her argument."

"What did she say to Chloe?"

"She said that Ben was a puck hog and needs to pass the puck more."

"Yeah, he does need to pass the puck more."

"Yeah. Whenever you have the puck on your stick, I think you should just skate with it, or pass it to Liam."

Danny's father lays a plate with four grilled cheese sandwiches in front of him. The smell of the gooey, buttery cheese lifts to Danny's nose.

"Ben got talked to by some scouts today."

"Really?" his father says.

"Yeah." Danny bites into his sandwich.

"And they didn't ask you?"

"Nope."

"You're kidding?"

Danny bites another gooey chunk out from his sandwich.

"Well," his father says. "Maybe you start being selfish on your line then."

"Yeah," Lexi says. "I don't think Ben deserves it any more than you do."

"You just gotta start scoring more goals, son!"

"If Ben leaves the team, then that would put you in a better position on the team for the rest of the season."

"But how would you feel about Ben then, Danny?" his father says. "Think you two would still be good buddies?"

"Why wouldn't we?" Danny says.

"He's most likely going to meet new kids on the higher up teams. He'll gain new friendships and he'll be taking things to a whole new level."

"Nah. We'll still be friends."

"I thought the same thing in high school," Lexi says. "When I was on the volleyball team, my best friend, Angelie, got promoted to the college team at the U. It took me a few weeks to realize that she didn't want to hang out with me anymore. She didn't want to be seen with me, never wanted to hangout in town. She only wanted to be with her college friends. So, that was the end of our friendship, and I haven't had the urge to talk to her since."

"But your girls, guys are more chill with it."

"Yeah, okay. We'll see about that."

SLEET

I pull up the driveway in my white SUV, creeping through the
pine trees that scatter the lawn. Snow blows with the strong winds
whistling through the tips of the pines. I catch a whiff of the little
tree freshener dangling from the rearview mirror. The warmth
from the heaters and the pizza I hadn't had too long ago makes me
sweaty in these hockey clothes. I want to go outside and plunge in
the blanket of fluff, but mom's probably wondering where I am. I
forgot to tell her that I went to Carbone's.

When I park the car and step out, the cold air refreshes my
skin. My body finally cools off after a long while of being in the
heat. I guess being a Minnesotan makes me love the cold, but it
can be a pain when the windows get frosted over the morning of a
school day. But we don't have school tomorrow, which is lit, or
else I'd have to scrape both the snow and ice that froze on my
windows overnight, or early in the morning for that matter.

I shuffle through the snow to the front door and walk inside.

As I seal the door shut, keeping the heat from escaping the house, my mom sets a novel down that she's reading on the coffee table in the living room. Bags have built under her eyes.

"Hey," she says. "You made it."

"Yep," says I. I lean on the wall that divides the front entrance to the living room. It's more of a supporting beam for the middle of the house. I suppose that's why it was there in the first place, and for a balanced look of course.

"Must have been a sluggish bus ride."

"Actually, I forgot to tell you. I was at Carbone's with Chester and Ash."

"I would have stayed up either way." My mom always stays up for me and waits till I arrive home. She wants to make sure I got home in one piece. It annoys me from time to time, but I guess I respect her point of view. "You had an amazing game!"

"Thanks."

"You really showed up Ben's and Danny's mom."

"Really? What'd they say?"

"Well, they were gossiping about how you got a penalty, and they said it basically affected the score of the game."

"Hm. That's funny."

"Sorry I left the game early."

"It's fine."

"I feel like it's not though."

"Mom, it's fine."

"No, it's not. I'm your mother." I keep my head down at the carpeted living room. "I can't bear it anymore, Liam. Every time I walk into a hockey rink, all I can think about is your dad."

My throat aches, and my stomach wants to churn but won't. My veins that connect from the back of my eye sockets to my brain rushes with blood. I didn't want to see my mom upset; it's too difficult for me. "Mom, I know. I'm sad about it too, but we have to move on. That was three years ago."

My mom looks out the window at the falling fluff, illuminated by the outside light. "I know, but it's still tough, Liam."

I need to change the conversation. I find something, but it isn't something I'm too thrilled to talk about. "Ben was spotted by a couple of scouts today."

"I thought those were scouts. They had their clipboards."

"Yeah. I saw them from the penalty box."

"Did they ask you or anyone else?"

"No. And I'm salty about it."

"Why are you salty about it?"

"I had my best game of the year, mom, and they never asked me. It feels like they didn't even recognize me, like they weren't even paying attention to the game."

"Well, score more goals. That's the only way you'll be recognized."

As much as it hurt to hear such a blunt answer from my mom, I know it's true. Scouts only look for the stats, and that's how you build an awful team. Let's just fill up our team with a bunch of self-centered puck hogs who only care about their ego more than the sport itself. But the teams that succeed are the ones with hard-driven passion, ones who want to play hockey for their strength, for their goals, for their mental health, for their skills, for the enjoyment. If you play hockey, it surely better not be for the enhancement of your ego, especially in high school. Everyone forgets about you anyways after high school, besides your clicky friends, and most kids don't move into college hockey because scouts only take the goal scorers these days. That's all they look for; they want a team that scores goals. But a team that really succeeds is a mixture of skills that can chemically combine into a beautiful recipe. You need the speed skater, you need the physically-active-in-the-gym, you need the track runner, you need the A student (but one who actually takes more difficult classes to challenge themselves), you need the goons . . . You need the boys who actually want to play hockey for a living! The ones who want to strive for their best in hockey and want to play hockey for the rest of their lives, they're the players you should be looking for. They're the most determined, they're the ones who challenge their strength in the weight room at five in the morning every morning, they're the ones who watch all the hockey clips to learn plays that worked and didn't work and they didn't just skip through the clips to watch THEIR best plays, they're the ones who don't care what line they play on, as long as they get an equal amount of playing time as everyone else on the team. They're the ones that you want, they're the ones who will burn the rust off their skates not for themselves, but for the team.

"I might go to the outdoor rink tomorrow," says I. "We don't have school."

"Oh," she says. "They cancelled it?"

"Yeah."

"Well, that would be great." She releases a howl yawn. "I think I'm going to hit the hay."

"Ok. Sounds good. Imma shower, then go to bed."

"Alright. See ya in the mornin."

SUNDOG

Danny unlocks the double set of french doors to The Barn. The snow from the storm flurries in the air, quieting down to its bitter end. He passes by the concession stand and walks into the Library of Skates; old rental skates that have been beaten with sticks, pucks, and just typical benders, line up the back wall like it's an ancient library bookcase. An outdated office counter is on the left when walking into the room, and it appears to mock a dentist office's front desk with double-decker counters. A separate room boxes out in the back-left corner behind the desk area. It looks like a small closet cell that has been pulled out from the wall. One would think it'd be used like a closet, but it's a closed-in space for the skate sharpener and skate oven. The door has been pulled off at one point to the closet as it's exposed to the rest of the room. Thin white blinds that were probably in an older suburban home beforehand covers the view to the outside flurries. There are two lights that shine in the ceiling tiles, giving the room a warm yellow haze inside.

Danny flicks two light switches on from behind the outdated office desk. The lights inside the hockey rink flicker on. They buzz with the electricity flowing through their veins. The ceiling fans slowly build up to half speed, ticking as only a few loose screws hold its verge of crashing onto the ice. The subzero temperatures seek through the thin sheet-metal walls of the arena. It's like one of those super early mornings where the boys have practice with the air just cold, dry, and groggy. But if coach brings sprinkled donuts, most of them will show up.

I told my mom that I was going to skate on the outdoor rink, which is what I'm doing, but it might be a pain in this cold weather. This morning, I had to scrape the tough ice that was glued to my windshield and passenger windows. Gotta love the brutal winters in Minnesota. But at least I love the outdoors. When I have a peaceful day with no hockey or school, I always try to venture out to a state park. I've been to so many around the state, even drove to one in western cheese-head state and South Dakota. Any state park with a frozen waterfall is one that I'd explore, besides the glories that settle around the Duluth area. It's a four-hour drive from Kielstad, and it sucks because all of Minnesota's true beauty lives up there. When we take a coach bus up to Duluth for a scrimmage, we never have the time to really explore Duluth the way that we want to, but I guess the true beauty of it all are the little memories with the boys. When we aren't competing for the top spot on the team, we actually feel like a little group of friends bonding with one another

I park my car in front of The Barn. Only one car coats in the snow, and I know it's Danny's. When you're on a team for a while, you learn each other's vehicles, so you know who's at the rink. It's just that little sense of clickiness inside us that seems to want to know who's here and who's not. I'd probably be more anxious if Ben and Cole were here with him, but he's alone. I guess that would make sense since he probably has to work the arena today. It's also not surprising to see Danny work on a super quiet day at the arena, most of the practices have probably been cancelled from the snowstorm.

When I open the door of my SUV, the flurries swift into the gap of my socks and sweatpants, landing right on my bare ankle. I leap onto the heaping fluff from last night's storm and bundle up in another one of my hockey hoodie sweatshirts. This sweatshirt is from junior year. It has our town's initials on the front left chest, and my last name and number is embroidered on the left arm sleeve. The dark grey color makes it a weird sweatshirt in my eyes, and it doesn't have a lot of insulation, but it'll do for the time being.

I lift my hoodie over my beanie hat and scurry to the double set of french doors of The Barn. The warmth inside wants to seep out into the cold like space vacuuming the inside of an exposed spaceship. It's tough to close the door with the warm air blowing outside, but I give all my umph in a strong pull and slam the door shut. The next set of french doors are much easier and pleasant to open. When I walk in, Danny walks from the Library of Skates to find me trampling in the snow on the clean rugs.

"Hey," Danny says. "What are you doin here?"

"I was gonna skate at the outdoor rink," says I.

"Really?"

"Yeah. I got nothing better to do today."

"The ice is packed with snow, dude."

"Oh yeah, guess I forgot about that."

"You're silly."

"It's okay though. I can shovel it up."

"Are you really gonna go out there? You can use the indoor ice. No one's using it."

"No, no. It's cool! I like being outdoors. Plus, I haven't used it yet and would like to."

"You have quite a winter left though."

"I know. If it's really bad out there, then I'll come back in and use the ice."

A thud comes from behind me. Ben walks in with his hockey warmups on.

"What's up," Danny says.

Ben budges his right shoulder in front of me and talks to Danny. Feels terrific to have a back facing towards me.

"I'm heading out to that scout practice," Ben says.

"Oh yeah, that's right," Danny says.

"Dude, I wish they would've asked you."

"Nah."

"Why wouldn't you want to take the opportunity?"

"I just don't have the time."

"Well, alright man. I gotta go get my gear and head out."

Ben pats Danny on the shoulder and leaves with his flat back. He flickers on the long hallway light and disappears around the corner.

"Is the shovel outside?" says I.

"Yeah," Danny says. "It should be leaning against the boards."

"Sweet! But yeah, I might come back in if it's too rough out there."

"Sounds good."

"And I may need a sharpening afterwards too."

"Yeah, I'll need one too. I'll wait for you then."

Danny heads out to the arena to resurface the ice with the morning coat. I head over to the long hallway to fetch up my skates from the locker room. There may be another awkward encounterment waiting for me in there.

THE SHED

A giant locker room fan dries our gear out from last night's game. Who knows where the fan came from, but it's one gigantic rusty beast. It's like one of those things where you call an ancient PC a dinosaur, or where an older television from the sixties would be considered out of date because of its boxy mass. This fan is the size of a shipping crate, and it spins quite vigorously. It'll rattle and shake when you turn it up to full power, but we always keep it on level one for a nice breeze in the locker room. But this morning is cold, not because of the temperature which has dropped under zero already, but the strange vibe I get from Ben inside of the locker room.

Luckily, the fan's on to produce some ambient noise. There's only me and Ben inside, and he hasn't said a word to me yet. I don't know if I should try to talk with him, I wouldn't even know what to talk about. We never just sit down and have a conversation about something. We've never been close to each other as teammates. He just feels like an enemy to me, like I have to compete with him all the time in tryouts, in practice, and in games. He's been glued to Danny all his life, and Cole eventually joined up with them in middle school. Dang, that was the beginning of clicky central. That's where all the popular kids decided to make friends with all the pro-athletes and gorgeous girls, then they shut everyone else out of their lives. No one gets in, and no one gets out. Usually, the non-athletic kids find all sportsy kids to be popular and well known, but hell, I'm an underdog. People know me as someone unique, someone different, like there's some sort of mystical power inside of me that just glows everywhere I go, but no one wants to be with the shining light. Am I just weird? What do I do that makes people not want to talk to me? They only talk to me when they need to, or at least that's what it seems to be. It just doesn't make sense, but then again, I tell myself, who cares! If these people don't talk to you, so be it. They're truly missing out on somebody who's going to be successful in life! I'm a senior in high school who has his shit together. I know what I'm going to do in my future. I'm going to make movies in my future. I thrive to make films, to write stories, to go beyond the imagination barrier and blow others' minds away. There's so much I want to tell people out in the world, but only so many will hear. I hope to reach that point in my life, I hope to be successful after one fricken hectic life, and let me tell ya, my boat ain't stopping soon. I may be directing my course on this lifeboat, but that propeller is never going to slow down. It keeps spinning and spinning and spinning, faster and faster and faster.

A ghostly chill sends trickles down my back. Goosebumps awaken on my arms and hairy legs. It's tough to hold back the shivers. I can't tell if it's from the breeze of the fan or from my anxiety with Ben in the room. He should hurry up, pack his stuff, and leave to his scout team. I'm still blown away by that, and of course, I'm salty about it. His parents probably just paid him onto the team. Danny didn't want to go, which is a good decision because we all know he didn't want to go anywhere with athletics. He's too lazy for that way of life. It's amazing to see so many fellow classmates in school and how little of them know what their future holds. They wait and they wait and they wait till one day, they notice they've been waiting for too long in life to receive absolutely nothing but stress. I thought I would go to school to become an astrophysicist, and later on, I would rocket off into the vastness of the Milkyway. So, my junior year of high school, I decided to take physics, which wasn't a required class for high school, but I had an idea for my future self. After junior year, I realized how painful physics was. This year, I take calculus for my math class, but I'm taking it just to experience it. But after that physics class, I studied myself, and I asked myself: Why did I want to be an astronaut so badly? Well, when I started to watch a lot of space movies, my mind was blown away. But what I didn't realize was that I loved their stories versus the beauty of it all. The stories almost persuaded me to reach my imaginations of becoming an astronaut. Now, I want people to read my stories, and I want them to embrace the critical messages I send to them before it's too late, especially teenagers. That is when life truly takes off for the stars.

Ben zips up his hockey bag and throws it over his shoulder. He closes the cubby to his stall and walks over to the stick stand to find his twig. It must be tougher to find his twig since him and all the other boys need matching tape jobs. They all need to have white tape, white helmet cages, and matching hockey gloves. Obviously, you need to look the part to fit the part, right? The door shuts behind him, and I can finally stop holding my breath. But I guess I didn't have to. He didn't dare to look at me once.

Maybe I should have taken Danny's offer on using the indoor ice. It would be nice to skate on smooth ice in the stale warmth of The Barn, but something pulls my mind to the outdoor rink. It could be because I love nature so much. I should have brought my GoPro with to shoot a hockey vlog on the outdoor rink, but I did want to spend my time working on my skills of shooting and stick handling. The thought of going outside to that rink though, it just gives me the strangest and most awkward vibe. My goosebumps are stiff, and my body tightens up in the shivering breeze.

I stand up to hopefully get the blood flowing through my body again. My beanie hat keeps my head in comfort. My hockey sweatshirt is warm, but my hockey jacket is quite thin, it may not do me much good out there. These sweatpants though, they are the bomb. The warmth of the thick fuzz wraps around my legs like a furry wolf's pelt. Hot chocolate is definitely gonna hit the spot after this.

I reach for my skates on the holders, which hang from the top of my stall. I grab my hockey gloves, then walk over to the stick stand to find my twig with torn up white tape and head out of the locker room.

The long hallway isn't any warmer, but at least the breeze is gone. Danny opened the arena not too long ago, and the heaters in The Barn take a century to heat up the whole place. The tin ceiling rattles from the wind outside, but the storm is calming. About a foot in a half of snow fell in the past couple of days. This'll be a good workout on the legs, and at least I'll get warmer from all the shoveling I look forward to doing (Minnesota sarcasm).

I take the shortcut out to the hockey rink and leave the long hallway and into the dryland room. The dryland room's dark, musty, and dusty. The bland morning light that shines through the overcast clouds and dying snow casts through the caged windows. The room feels even colder than the locker room with the flat white light coming from outside. I hesitate to open the door to the outdoor rink, but I'm gonna have to shovel sooner or later. Might as well get it done now then let the time drift away. Besides, I'll be sweating before I know it.

When I open the hefty steel door, a twirl of wind whips snow inside of the dryland room. The cold turns the fresh snow into this powder, and this powder is annoying when it seeps inside of your socks and shoes. It's a good thing there's The Shed right next to the outdoor rink. It's aged its way through storms like this, and it has a heater, takes a while to heat up but faster than heating up The Barn. My father used to skate out here with his friends all the time when he was a teenager, but he'd never let us have outdoor practice in Bantams on that sheet of ice. I could never understand why.

I shuffle through the powdery snow as my feet sink deeper and deeper with every step. The snow is so high that my kneecaps bury into the snow. On the bright side, hockey players are great with hard strides, even when your legs feel like steel artillery that were used on older World War II submarines. Pushing through this snow is no challenge for me, but it might be tougher for Danny.

The Shed's door is cracked open for the slightest wisp of wind to sneak inside. I push the door open and immediately lean against its back, fighting the wind till it flushes shut. When I flick the light switch on, the electrical lines along the ceiling spark the lights to life. I find the heater on the far side attached to the ceiling. The switch is tricky to reach, but the twig is more than just a sniper. I grasp the handle of my twig and use the blade of the stick to reach the top of the heater, which is so difficult with the ceiling and the heater almost kissing each other. But I shove my stick between the gap and feel the slight indent of the switch. The heater ticks, the fan spins, and its metallic veins glow red.

While the heater kicks in, I might as well get outside and shovel. I set my gear down on a bench. Another door sits by a bigger window, and it overlooks the outdoor rink and the side of The Barn. Some pine trees sway in the wind to the left of the rink. The ends of the outdoor rink have chained-link cages you'd find on a baseball field. Two outdated stadium lights tower over the rink on opposite corners. The boards cover in black puck marks, and some of the white has been ripping off the wood for decades.

An old zamboni is specially used for this outdoor rink, but it barely comes out to resurface the ice. It may come out about every other week, when it's functioning that is.

As I look out the window, my mind drifts away from the idea of skating out here. Danny was right. With this much snow, it's gonna take a long time before I can get any skating in. By the time I shovel all this off, I won't have the energy or muscle power to even work on my skills.

While I bend down to the bench to grab my gear, my eyes draw in on a message that was engraved into the white wooden wall. Some sort of maroon substance is in the engravement. Dry blood possibly, old and rotten dry blood. I take my pointer finger and feel the bumps in the white wood. The first letter has two long towers with a straight bridge connecting them. Next, this letter appears to be a diving platform you'd find in a competitive swimming pool, it has two . . . no . . . three diving platforms on it, then the last two things were symbols . . . they were hockey sticks, not crisscrossed like chel but standing and facing the same direction, blades pointing down and to the right. It isn't long till I understand the message. What other four-letter word would have double hockey sticks at the end of it? The message, it read:

H E |_ |_

The message brings a strange vibe. One would think it's cute, but it looks to have been made with fingernails. Why would anyone want to do that to themselves?

Before I leave, I need to turn the heater off. Here we go again with the tricky configuration, but man this twig is handy. I flick the switch off as it ticks its glowing veins away. I head over to the bench again to grab my skates off the ground. The lights flicker before shutting off on me. The silence sinks deeper and deeper into my mind as the darkness from the back of The Shed taunts me. I walk to the door I came through, but before I leave, I notice something through the window. There's some sort of steam or fog arising from the snow that covers the ice. I turn around and go through the second door, then I encounter the chained-link gate. I lift the handle of the gate and pull it open as the metal hinges squeak in the forbidden wind. My feet plop down in the powdery snow. The steam arises from center ice. I shuffle through the snow to find the steam melting all the snow that surrounds it. When I cross the blue line, or assuming the blue line is near me, I look over the hills of snow and notice what the steam is coming from.

Blood. Fresh dry blood burns through the ice, and it has been bleeding for a while now. It's so near to drowning into the dirt beneath it. I'm shocked the blood hasn't froze in the ice, but it doesn't make sense why there's blood outside. Was there a hockey game out here? Maybe there was a big brawl between two guys? I don't know, but I want to head inside and get me some hot chocolate. I turn around to find my path I skidded through. The dry blood trails to The Shed. It's like the blood is coming back to life or something, or maybe there's pipes running underground that's heating the ground and melting the ice and blood away.

As strange as the morning is, more blood only made mine run colder.

SNAP

The wind gusts down Main Street as Ash enters Snap, which is not
too far from Flippers, only a few blocks down the street. The
gym's empty. No surprise there. Usually, there would be a few
younger adults jogging on the treadmills, and a few football guys
would be lifting weights, but the storm must have scared them
away. At least it's a decent excuse to not workout for a few days,
but something bugs Ash's mind. He does workout at Snap quite a
bit to beef up those muscles though, then he can wear his tank top
wherever he goes and feel confident with it on.

The humidity sticks to the skin like a thick, milky slab of
peanut butter. There's also the traditional smell of rubber from the
mats that surface the floor and the plates used for squats, bench,
and clean. On the left, near the window that looks out to Main
Street, shoe cubbies stack along the wall, and a mini fridge
contains mini waters for the membership holders. There's a ramp
that leads to another room, behind the wall of treadmills. The

room in the back is used for yoga, but Ash puts the room to good use with his ab workouts too.

He pulls off his hoodie and wears a t-shirt with ripped off sleeves, mimicking a tank top. He keeps his sweatpants on and throws his hoodie, car keys, and wallet inside the cubby. The televisions and fans along the wall of mirrors, right in front of the treadmill machines, oscillate some background noise. Ash pops in some headphones and cranks the volume up. A steady beat of drums blare out as a rapper cusses out his traumatic breakup.

Ash walks down the open aisle between the treadmills, which are on his left, and the stationary bikes, which are on his right. Behind the bikes sit the weightlifting machines. The squat rack is down, near the far wall that aligns with dumbbells ranging from ten pounds to a hundred-and-twenty. As he walks by the mirrors, the parallax world copies his moves. The meteorologist discusses the cold temperatures that hold through the rest of the week on two of the three televisions, the other one replays the Minnesota Wild game that must have been on the other night, which they probably lost, what a shocker. The treadmills bore in their stillness, all but one. One of the treadmills towards the back moves at the speed of 0.4. It barely slides along but yet you can just barely see it. Ash doesn't even recognize it. He focuses on his music and preps for his bench.

He reaches the rack and stretches out his arms; a few arm stretches across the chest, toe touches to pull the back muscles, and then arm swings to loosen up. He grabs a forty-five plate from the right of the bar. He slides the plate on the bar, then grabs the lock and tightens the plate in place. The right side is set, and he now moves to the other side and does the same thing. A forty-five-pound plate slides on the bar and grips in place with the firm lock.

It's time to bench.

Ash lays his back upon the cushioned seat that appears to be comfortable but isn't as comfy as it looks. He positions his boney spine on the hard, flat seat, feeling every rivet and bump on it. His hands raise up to grasp the bar. They squeeze on and off till he finds the right spot. He shuts his eyes, then heaves in a deep breath of sticky air. The air blows out of his mouth, some saliva included, as he lifts the bar off its resting stand. All the weight hovers above his chest with his arms straightened out and his focus sharp on the ceiling.

Ash drops the bar and takes another deep breath in. The bar touches his chest, then he pushes it off with a burst of energy. The bar raises up, and then back down. Back up. Back down. Back up. Back down. He continually pumps the bar up and down with acceleration. His arms slow down on him, and he sets the bar back on its shelf. He allows his arms to dangle to the side. Sweat from his forehead streams down his red cheeks.

He sits up, catches his breath, then reloads the bar with twenty more pounds on each side. Once he locks them in place with the grips, he lays back on his boney spine. He prepares his grip on the bar, bouncing his hands on and off to find that perfect spot. One breath in, one breath out. He raises the bar off its rest and benches again. The speed of the bar pumps up and down, faster and faster and faster. Ash grunts with every lift, louder and louder as he goes. More sweat streams down from his scalp, some rolling down the back of his neck. One drip of sweat itches at his back, but he ignores the temptation to stop and scratch at it. His arms slow down, and his last few pumps look weak, but he manages to push the bar up with one final roar, throwing the bar back on its shelf.

After a few seconds of rest, Ash reloads his bar with more weight. He adds on another ten pounds to each side. The bar now weighs a hefty one-hundred-and-ninety-five pounds. He locks the weights in and returns to the uncomfortable rubber seat. His shoulders burn, and his arms are wimpy worms dangling off a fishing hook. His hands rise up to the bar and tighten around the sweet spot. One breath in, one breath out. The bar lifts off its rest and hovers for a moment. With a deep inhale, Ash pumps in fury. Gravity takes the bar down and drops it to the tip of his chest, then he pushes it away from him, wanting to throw it at the ugly white ceiling tiles above him. He pushes the bar, faster and faster, harder and harder. His sweat floods his face and greases the seat from under him. The bar slows down while Ash feels weak, but he thinks he can get a few more pumps in. He struggles to get one up, but he gets it. He goes for one more. The bar drops to his chest. He explodes in a ferocious scream as he lifts the bar up halfway up to its rest point. The bar now moves as slow as the treadmill moves from behind him, but it stops and drops back down onto Ash's chest. He closes his eyes as his head limps to the side. He's stuck.

A whimper leaks out from Ash's salty lips. He stenches of sweat from the pits; deodorant never seems to help. Sweat flows more streams down the side of his head. He just lies there upon his bumpy spine, resting on an uncomfortable rubber seat as his exhaustion cools his body down.

Ash's phone vibrates in his pocket. He looks down by his legs and notices the safety ramps on the side, meant more for squats, but they were in line with his seat. So, he scurries out from under the bar, his sweat on the seat acting like butter which helps slip him out. The bar drops down on the safety ramps. He lays on the floor and checks his phone.

A text message from Coach Kipp reads: Practice will still be on today at 4:00pm.

He sets the phone aside, rests his hand against his forehead, and lays down with his salt.

TORRID

After seeing all that blood on the outdoor rink, I trudge through the deep snow and to the french doors of The Barn. Finally, the heat soaks through the skin at my fingertips. My feet will soon be soaked with melted snow. It'd be nice to get my feet heated by something, but something cold stands in my mind. I may be in the heat now, but shivers still trickle down my back, like water melting off an icicle, then the water drips off from the icicle and down the back of your shirt. It's amazing how just one little drop can bother someone.

Danny pops out from the concession stand. A fresh salted pretzel holds in one hand with gooey nacho cheese in the other. It's pretty typical that he doesn't use a plate or even a paper towel for his food. But the steam that arises from the hot cheese makes my mouth melt with rich gooeyness. Fresh hot food sounds amazing. I can use some heat inside my belly.

"Hey," Danny says. "Changed your mind?"

"Yeah," says I. "I think I'll use the indoor ice."

"I'm about to sharpen my skates here. Do you want yours sharpened?"

"Might as well."

"Do you want them baked?"

"That would be awesome actually. My feet are in glaciers right now." I hand over my beat-up skates to him. The laces dangle off with the tips looking like they've been chewed on.

"I'll get started on yours. Do you actually mind getting mine from the locker room?"

"Oh, sure. I can get em."

Danny walks my skates into the Library of Skates. I start to make my way over to the long hallway. I look down at my shoes which squishes out puddles onto the rubber mats. When I turn the corner to the long hallway, I gradually look up to find the dangling caged lights swinging in the silence. They're not swinging immensely, but it's like a swing at a playground gently pushed upon by the wind. Every other light swings in a pattern; One swings right left right, the one behind it swings left right left, and so on down the excruciating long hallway.

I move down the hall with the lights swinging above me, passing them one by one. The dryland room appears to my left. The shadows of the pines by the outdoor rink cast their silhouettes through the caged windows. Their shadows abnormally spin in circles on the ground. It's almost like when you get knocked out during a game, maybe like a blackout, where the whole room just spins around you. Or it's like when your iron deficiency is low, and there's that sudden moment of dizziness. I feel like I'm on a spinning spaceship watching these shadows disorientate my balance.

I continue down the long hallway of swinging caged lights. The heat in the duct rumbles a deep ambience and echoes as if it were a tunnel. But the heat slowly dies off the further I make it down the hall. My feet are freezing into thicker glaciers and my fingers lose their warmth. The only thing that makes me feel safe is my beanie hat. Its comfort squeezes lightly around my head.

The dizziness comes back. I fall forward into my walk but catch myself, shoving my arms into the walls. I give my head a second to spin itself out. The maroon stripe on the wall waves all the way down the hallway like ocean waves. Now I feel sick to my stomach. Some food would do some good, or maybe some water. I don't know, it hurts too much to think.

My brain takes in a second wind. The spinning stops. I speed walk down the hallway and pass the swinging lights. The locker room is just a few more steps away. I get to the door and walk inside. The lights click on with its sensor picking up my movement. Basically, the light has a red eye that stares into the vast darkness of space until it picks up movement, then it falls asleep. It's only awake when the room is empty.

Once I pass the stick stand in the entrance of the locker room, I search for Danny's nametag on the stalls. He sits on the left side; that's where all the cool kids sit. Coach Kipp has his own coach's locker room, but he never lets anyone inside. All I know is that the door is a little further down the long hallway, and it has its own mini hallway forked off from the long one. I always wonder what's in there, but he just says he needs his own space.

Danny's skates hang on the drying holders from the top of the stall. One day, a skate is just gonna collapse off those sticks and hit someone on the head. Danny can use a little knocking on the head, or Ben. At least Danny is doing me a favor. Ben would never ask me something like that, ever. The only time he would do something for me is if I tell him to do it, but even that's a fifty-fifty shot.

Before the dizziness arrives again, I hustle with Danny's skates over to our locker room's bathroom sink. I twist the faucet on with the blue dot, cup my hands, and chug down the water I collect. Sink water does not taste the best, especially this dirty well water, but when you're gasping for air on the bench, any water is gold to a player. The water refreshes my face as it splashes sprinkles at me.

I twist the faucet off and leave the locker room with his skates. The lights swing and the ambient vent rumbles. Some heat pushes on me as it flows down the hallway, but the temperature seems to flex from warm to cold, then warm to cold again. Finally, The Barn starts to cozy up. I walk down the long hallway and glance my eyes into the dryland room. The shadows rotate through those caged windows and onto the floor.

I tell myself to keep moving. Danny's probably wondering where I'm at with his skates. I turn the corner and made it back. The smell of that pretzel coats my brain with its gooey cheese. It sounds so delightful right now. Maybe Danny will let me make one. I head into the Library of Skates as sparks fly out from the little corner closet. Nothing beats the natural sound of a skate sharpener.

A chair hides in the corner by the wall of skates. I take a seat and set Danny's skates down by my side. My head falls to my shoulder as my eyes droop shut. For a moment, it doesn't even feel like I have control of my body. It just wants to shut down and relax.

"Tired?" Danny says. I burst open my eyes to find Danny grabbing his skates by my side.

"A little bit," says I.

"I just put your skates in the oven. They should be ready in like ten minutes."

"Okay." I think to ask him for a pretzel, but I hesitate not to ask in this current state. "Danny. Do you mind if I make myself something?"

"In the concessions? Yeah, go ahead!"

"Thank you."

He moves back into the tucked-away corner closet to sharpen his skates. I leave the Library of Skates and into the concession stand. Neon lights pop out from the Pepsi machine on the far-left corner. An island of candy choices is in the middle of the kitchen. To my direct left is a white fridge and deep freezer. Ripped cardboard from ice cream and popsicle boxes were taped onto them. An empty pizza machine stands in the far back corner, next to the stand that holds the chip bags with clips. To the right of that, there is the popcorn machine, coffee machine with choices of french vanilla and hot chocolate, hot dog rotator, and then the pretzel machine with its nacho cheese dispenser. A microwave hides to my right in the corner, next to the steel farm sink.

I grab a paper plate from the counter. Opening the top freezer compartment of the white fridge, I take a frozen pretzel out from the bag. Some of the snow crystals from the bag grasp onto my skin. I place the hard-twisted bread on the paper plate and rest it inside the microwave. The timer has a button for frozen food, so I push that one. The light flares up inside and the turntable spins.

In the meantime, I might as well get my nacho cheese. A stack of little black plastic cups stands right next to the cheese dispenser. I pump the cheese in a black cup with the dispenser's handle. When the microwave beeps its head off, I pop the door open and touch my warm, squishy pretzel. I take the spray bottle from the top of the microwave and spray the water on the pretzel. The salt hides on the other side of the machine. I sprinkle salt onto the moist pretzel. I leave the concession stand with my watering taste buds and walk back to my seat in the Library of Skates.

Danny finishes his skates with the last set of sparks flying back from the corner closet. He walks out with his skates, sets them on the old office desk, and reclines back in the office chair. I dip a chunk of the salted pretzel into the nacho cheese, then devour it and savor its salty, gooey warmth.

"How's the pretzel?" Danny says.

"Amazing," says I.

"Did you see coach's text?"

"No?" I pull out my phone with a message sent from coach.

"He's still having practice on today."

"Really?"

"Yeah, it's fucking dumb."

The time sticks out from the message and reads: 4pm. "It's in a few hours too."

"Can't we just have one day off."

"Yeah. To be honest, that'd be nice."

Ting!

Danny lifts off from his seat. "Welp, your skates are done." He walks into the corner closet to the oven, which sits to the left of the skate sharpener. The red numbers on the oven spike in a steady climb. The temperature reads 425, then 435, 445, 460, 480, 520, 560, 610 . . . The numbers continue to rise. Danny stares at it for a while, shocked by the machine. He opens the door to the oven and slowly moves his hand inside. He places the tip of his finger on the skate, and his finger lies on the skate for a few seconds. Then, he grasps the bottom of the skates and takes them out. When he closes the door to the oven, the red numbers power off.

He brings the skates over to me and sets them on the floor.

"Alright," he says. "You'll keep these on for fifteen, then your skates will be set."

"Sounds good." I put the pretzel on the counter, then throw my shoes off. I grab the first skate, unlace the laces that Danny must have tightened, and tug out on the tongue. The left skate squeezes around my left foot, and then the right skate squeezes onto my right foot. The warmth of the fuzzy interior comforts my soaked socks. I pull on the laces till the skate feels firm, locking my feet in place, just like some newbies would do so they don't appear as a bender, but they always do no matter how tight the skates are. I finish tightening my laces with a double knot. Both skates are locked and firm.

I reach for my pretzel and take it off the counter. I lean back in my chair and rip another chunk of bread off it. When I dip it into the cheese and munch on it, my eyes draw over to the first aid box behind Danny. It hangs on the wall with a red cross on it. This triggers something back that I want to bring up to him.

"Hey, Danny," says I. "Did something happen at the outdoor rink the other day?"

"Ummmmm," he says. "I'm not sure. I wasn't on duty."

"Oh, okay."

"Why?"

"Well, when I shoveled some snow off the ice, there was some blood on it."

"Yeah, not the first time it's happened."

"Yeah, but like, there was A LOT of blood on it."

"Someone probably just had a nosebleed or something."

"But something weird was happening to it."

"Like what?"

"The blood . . . it was so fresh. It was like melting through the ice. I could see the steam arising from it. And it kept melting through the ice and into the ground, then I found the trail of blood . . . I don't know, it's just odd."

"Huh. I have no clue what happened." Danny grabs a pen from the desk. He looks at it with inspiration. He pops the cap off and it bounces onto the floor. He bends down and picks it up. I look at his hand as he sets it on the counter. It's shaking. He pulls himself up to the desk and writes on a sheet of paper.

A drop of sweat streams down the side of my cheek. The room seems to be heating up. I take my beanie hat off and toss it under my seat. Then, I pull my hockey sweatshirt off and toss it on top of my beanie hat. My hand swipes the sweat off from my cheek, but another drip of sweat rolls down the other side of my face, and then another.

"Hey, Danny," says I. Danny continues to write on the sheet. "I hate to bother, but could you get me some water?"

"Sure," he says. He walks out of the room. I watch him walk into the concession stand.

These skates are giving me a hot flash. The room feels like a sauna; hot, thick, and moist like a jungle. My skin feels sticky while my scalp begins to irritate me. I scratch it out. Then, it seems like a tiny spider crawls along my back. I smack at it. It's gone. But then another one crawls from under my sweatpants. I scratch it out, and it's gone. A few more itches crawl along my arm, then my back again. More drips of sweat fall from my curly black hair. I tug my shirt away from my chest to air out the sweat. It's beginning to dampen my athletic shirt.

Where's Danny with my water? I want to pull these skates off.

I grasp the left skate's lace with my fingers, but it sticks to my fingers like syrup. I pull my fingers away as it stretches out the lace like taffy. A burning sensation from the lace reddens my fingers. I try to pull my other skate's lace but more of it sticks to my hand. The wax on the laces are melting. I attempt to pull the left skate off my foot, but it won't budge off. I can't get any wiggle room in there. It squeezes on my foot like a blood pressure cuff at its tightest grasp, and it actually feels like it's getting tighter by the second. My foot burns a bit, just like when showering and the water is piping hot. It's like a cold sensation with a sting in it. I'm feeling that same sting on both my feet. But now it's getting hotter, and hotter, and hotter, and there's more stinging all around my feet. A bunch of needles stab into my foot, digging down into the bone. I can't tell if the wetness inside is still from the melted snow or if blood's seeping out. I pull and pull and pull at my skate, but it isn't budging one bit.

I can't help but whimper, "Danny!"

He walks out from the concession stand with a bottle of water. He looks down at my feet. Smoke and steam arise from my skates. I see the smoke and steam as a swarm of stingers stab into my feet, digging into the surface of my skin.

"DEAR GOD, HELP ME, DANNY!"

He stands there with the water shaking in his hand, staring at my skates.

I burst out another scream as blood seeps out from my skates, bubbling. Millions of needles sting down to the bone. I try ripping the skates off, but they burn my hands with its sticky exterior. More smoke and steam arise from my feet.

One of the french doors bangs shut. Ben walks in beside Danny.

"HELP ME!" I want to cry, but my eyes are so dry.

Ben hustles over and grasps the bottom of my skates. It burns his hands as he jumps back.

"PLEASE HELP ME!"

Ben looks around the room and finds a pair of hockey gloves on the floor by the wall of skates. He slides them on. He grasps a tight grip around the bottom of my right skate. He pulls with all his might. The bottom of the skate stretches off while the top of the skate stays stuck to my ankle. I can see my toes burning in the melting rubber, and I can also see a little white of the bone from my big toe. Ben moves to my left skate and again, the bottom half pulls away like stretchy syrup.

I scream out my lungs again with the burns and stings seeping deeper and deeper to the bone. Ben takes his sticky gloves and rips off the top portions of my melting skates, like a dog pawing into the ground to bury something in the dirt. I can feel my feet freeing into the air, but the pain isn't going away. My feet appear to be made of tar as the blood boils on my skin from the burning rubber.

I whimper and whimper in pain. I look up to the ceiling, wanting to die and live in peace. Get me out of this Hell. I slowly look down at Ben, his eyes point to my blood that boils down into the rubber mat. He stops ripping away at the rubber. He just stares and stares at the boiling blood. A lightbulb bursts inside of my head, sending shards of glass through my brain.

"Oh my God," says I. "It was you!"

Ben paws again at the skate chunks that stick to my feet, but he looks up at me. I look down at him, then back at Danny.

"It was both of you!"

Ben stops. He digs into my eyes with his, then he stands up and goes to Danny.

"Did you tell him?" Ben says. Danny just shakes in shock. "TELL ME!" Danny's still. Ben hurries towards me and picks me up. He takes me over by Danny and hangs on to me. "Danny. Get your keys, now!"

Danny grabs the keys off the office desk and follows me and Ben down to the long hallway. My head dangles off Ben's arms while I stare up at the dangling caged lights. They violently swing from wall to wall. A few blink on and off. The ducts roar with energy and shake from the ceiling supports above. It's so deliquiate to watch the lights swing side to side, so mesmerizing.

Ben bangs open the game doors at the end of the long hallway. Ben walks me inside of the zamboni room. He drops me from his arms. I fly for less than a second, then my head slams and bounces off the concrete floor. My voice feels dead inside.

"Danny," Ben says. "Give me the zamboni keys and unbolt the cage."

Ben leaps onto the zamboni seat as Danny pulls the chain to the steel garage door. Ben drives the zamboni onto the ice in reverse and parks it. Danny finds a drill on the tool shelf along the wall. He begins to unbolt the metal frame that lies on the floor. That's where the snow from the ice would settle into after resurfacing, it's a mucky pit. Ben walks in, and Danny takes off the last bolt. Ben looks down at me while I lie on the floor in some comedic pain.

"I should have known!" He stares at me. "That's Finn's blood outside, isn't it?" Ben's fists clench up, and his jaw tightens. "You killed him!"

"WE DIDN'T KILL HIM!"

"BULLSHIT!"

Ben digs his hand through my sweatpants' pockets. He steals my phone. Danny pulls the metal cage off from the pit. Ben squats down and picks me off the cold concrete. I scream out my last might as he throws me into the small snow pile down inside of the pit. Danny and Ben pull the metal cage over the pit, then Danny starts on the bolts.

"What are you gonna do to me!" says I.

"Yeah," Danny says. "What are we doing, Ben? This is fucking crazy."

"You want him to tell the world that we killed Finn?" Ben says.

"We didn't though!"

"I know! But right now, he thinks otherwise! At least this way we can talk to him without him running off. But first, we need to talk!"

Ben walks out. The zamboni engine props on. I can hear the wheels crunching along the dirty concrete. Darkness fades over me as Ben drives the zamboni over the cage.

"No!" says I. "Don't leave me here!"

The chain of the garage door rattles as the door seals shut. They walk out of the zamboni room and leave me in the darkness. The warm yellow light from above the zamboni fades into the pit.

THE PENALTY

The walls that surround me are pitch black. A drop of oil lands on my hand. It's dripping from the zamboni.

"Liam," a voice whispers.

I look into the darkness. Nothing. Absolutely nothing.

CHEL

Chester games on his console in his bedroom. He sits on a gaming chair made of black leather. Two speakers come out of the sides of the head rest, and the bass woofer is on the back. A black controller busies his fingers as a whistle blows through the chair. He's playing Chel. The puck is about to drop in the offensive zone with half a minute remaining in the third, and it's a tie game between his Minnesota Wild and the Toronto Maple Leafs, 3-3. It's the final game in the Stanley Cup finals. Both teams are three and three.

This is the biggest moment of the year in the hockey world. That Stanley Cup may just be a tin cup, but there's a means of power, dedication, hard work, and passion inside it, and when a team of boys can hold a trophy together, then they are more than just a team, they are brothers living inside of their destined dreams.

The referee drops the puck while Chester pushes the Leaf's

centerman and ravages for it. He kicks the puck back with his skates to his left defensemen who's along the boards. The left defenseman fires the puck to the high center where his partner loads up for a slap shot. The Leaf's left-winger glides up the ice with his knees pushed in, ready for a suicide block. Chester fakes the slapshot, then slides it over to the left defensemen again.

Twenty seconds left in the period.

Chester sneaks a bump pass off the boards to his low-side wing, standing on the hashmarks. He one-touches it to the same defensemen. Left defensemen fires the puck over to the right defensemen. He shoots it down to the right winger, sliding over to the other faceoff circle and along the boards. Right winger finds his centerman low in the corner. They crisscross each other and switch positions. He backhands the puck to the centerman who passes it right back to right defenseman. Chester fires the puck over to the left defensemen. The left defenseman raises his stick up to his waist, loads his back leg with power, then pounds the puck at the net while his stick flexes against the ice. The puck frisbees in between the Leaf's centerman and defenseman while Chester's left-winger pushes the centerman out of the way. The goalie reaches for the puck with his blocker, but the puck flies right by his head and hits the sweet spot; post and in. With the ring of the post, the lighthouse spins its light and blares its train horn. Everyone jumps up from their seats, including Chester.

Nine seconds left in the third period. 4-3.

The Wild roll through their line of handshakes. Chester keeps the same line out for the final seconds of this championship game.

Towels from around the stadium twirl as the crowd roars for these final moments. The referee skates up to Chester and the Leaf's centerman. He drops the puck. Chester ties up the centerman, then protects the puck in between his skates. His left-winger sneaks his blade from under him and takes the puck. He skates it into their defensive zone while the crowd finishes the countdown. The lighthouse celebrates with its horn and light, and Chester jumps with the players and the crowd on screen. They just won the Stanley Cup. He just won the Stanley Cup.

That wonderful tingling sensation trimmers down his back, then his arms, and then his legs. His hairs stick up from the goosebumps along his body. Oh, how great would it be to win the state championship in the High School Hockey Tournament! It's every player's dream, but only so little make it in. Chester knows that it'd be tremendous to go to state and to play in the Exel Energy Center while the game is broadcasted around the world with everyone watching, but he also knows how little our chance is to make it through playoffs. There's not enough dedication on this team, not enough pushers, only ego-fishing boys.

Chester pulls out his phone and calls someone. He walks over to his window and pulls the blind up. When he looks out, past the neighbor's house and a few other suburban homes, he notices a break in the clouds. The sun blasts its white headlights like from a car at night, blinding the drivers on the country roads. But it isn't just one sun, there are three suns. The other two are smaller but shine just as bright. It's a cyclops' eye with two dimples, but it wouldn't be smiling, it appears more like a frown. Minnesota receives many sundogs in the cold mornings, some people like them because they think its luck for their day, and then others despise of the natural occurring phenomenon as it blinds them on the roads. But yes, it's totally acceptable to wear sunglasses in the snowy winter.

The other side of the phone clicks on. "Hello?"

"Hey, Ash!" Chester says.

"Hey," he says. "What's up?"

"I didn't wake you, did I? I guess I forgot you like to sleep in."

"No, no. I've been up for a while, just chillin on my bed right now."

"Well, I was wondering if you would like to come over and play some Chel with me, or just hangout before practice?"

"We have practice? Fuck! Umm . . ." Ash thinks about this for a few seconds. "Sure."

"Okay, sweet! You can come over whenever you're ready, and maybe I can call Liam too and see if he wants to join." Ash seems to have fallen asleep on the other side. "Ash?"

"Oh, sorry. Yeah, I guess that'd be fine."

"You don't sound too thrilled about it?"

"Well, why does Liam have to be with?"

"What do you mean?"

"Can't it just be the two of us?"

"I mean, yeah. It could just be the two of us, but why don't you want Liam here?"

"I— I don't know. He's kind of bugging me right now, like

he's a little annoying."

"How so?"

"I just feel like he gets all the attention."

"What?"

"Like why didn't I get any attention from the Dorcha game? Why are my parents the only ones telling me what a good game I had? Coach doesn't even like me."

"Coach only likes his first liners."

"And Liam! He's like his pet."

"Ash, look. I don't receive a lot of attention either. And let's be honest, we all know Coach Kipp can be subjective. But with Liam, I mean, fuck dude, his dad died. His fucking dad is dead. I honestly don't know what goes on inside his mind, he never wants to talk about the past, but I can only imagine the Hell he has gone through these last years." Ash sniffles some snot up his nose. "You know how awesome his dad was as a coach. He never got pissed when we lost a game, disappointed, but never pissed. He knew what we needed. All we really wanted to do in squirts, peewees, and bantams, is play some good ol hockey!" Chester presses his hand against some frost on the border of the window. The heat from his hand melts the frost as a drip streams down it.

"I wish things were like they were!" Ash says. "Liam and I always hung out with each other. I remember our road trip up to Roseau in our last year of Bantams. My dad drove our soccer mom van with Liam and his dad with us. I brought my console for the five-hour trip and we gamed Chel all the way up."

Silence.

Chester takes his hand off the cold window while more drops of water stream down the glass. "I'm with ya, bud. I don't want to grow up."

"That was the life. Those were the best times of my fucking life!"

"And I know Liam thinks the same way, Ash. He's just living a tough life right now too. But we need to be there for him, always! He needs us! We don't need another man down on this team. You hear me?"

Ash blows his nose into a Kleenex. "Yeah."

"Promise me. Promise me that you'll be there for Liam no matter what."

"I promise."

"Okay. And you know I'll always be here for you, Ash. Liam too. We're brothers after all, aren't we?"

"Of course!"

"Okay. Why don't you start getting ready and head on over here? I'll call Liam and see what he's doing."

"Okay."

"Alright then." Chester pulls his phone away from his ear.

"Wait, Chester!"

"Yeah?"

"Thank you!"

"I love you, bud."

"I love ya too!"

Chester hangs up, then dials another number. He stands by the window, watching the clouds drift upon the sundog. The phone rings and rings its monotone hum, all the way to voicemail. Chester calls another number in hope for a pickup.

Mother sizzles her strips of bacon on a frying pan while the wall phone clangs on its hanger. She licks her greasy fingers, dries them on the towel that hangs from the oven's door handle, then walks to the wall phone and picks it up. "Hello?"

"Hi, this is Chester."

"Hey, Chester! Are you calling for Liam?"

"Yeah. I was wondering if he'd like to hang out at my place before practice."

"Oh, so you guys do have practice today."

"Yep. Coach kept it on."

"Well, he's skating at the outdoor rink. I don't know when he'll be back. Did he not answer his phone?"

"No. But that's okay. Ash and I are hanging out soon and maybe we'll join him."

"Yeah, that sounds great to me."

"Sounds good. Thank you!"

"No problem, darling. Bye-bye, now."

VEINS

It's too dark beyond the cold concrete wall. I think I'm hearing things, maybe I'm going crazy. Is this what pure depression feels like? I mean, I have days where I'm upset, days where I cry and cry and cry for hours upon hours, no sleep while my brain constantly chugs along, but then I have those days where I'm back to normal, nothing special though. I don't know the last time I've been happy. Senior year kills me, and out of all the years of my suffering, why is senior year feeling out of place?

The filthy snow now rests over the center drain like a salt pile. Can't seem to tell time without a watch, my cellphone, or inside an underground prison for all that matter. There's nowhere to escape from this cellar. The hefty metal cage is bolted shut, no ones in The Barn to call out for, unless Ben and Danny have a sudden change of heart.

A crack echoes through in the darkness of the concrete wall. I lean my head against it, flattening my ear to its cold, stale base.

Another crack, almost like someone cracking their hand, but it isn't a normal hand, their hand would have to be double jointed for it to crack that much. It's probably just some old pipes crackling from under the ice. Or at least I believe that's the way I'm facing. I move from the wall to see which direction I'm facing. The mop of the zamboni directs me to the ice. Must just be the ice crackling like Rice Krispies.

But the cracks get louder and louder. Something is inching towards me. I crab walk my way back from the wall till my hands flush down into the snow pile. I wrap my arms around my legs and squeeze my head into my chest. The crackling closes in on my ears, ripping my anxiety into shreds and whipping them all over.

With one excruciating crack, everything turns silent. Whatever it is, I know it's standing in front of me. I'm not alone in the cellar. If I look, it'll be just like the nightmare I had with dad. But I have to look. The silence kills me. If I keep my eyes covered, someone's gonna end up yelling into my ears.

I lift my head from out of my chest. I peek out from my eyelids. I don't see anything in front of me. Now, I'm safe to open my eyes. My eyes focus on the dark, more and more and more. The dim light that the zamboni protrudes melts away as the darkness seems to grow around me. But something begins to reveal itself from the darkness of the concrete wall. It doesn't look too terrifying, but who the hell would be down here. No one, absolutely no one. Its feet and kneecaps appear more vivid as my eyes focus; the toes frostbit, the kneecaps pale white. The legs move into a kneeling position. A pale white hand delicately moves and flattens against the surface of the concrete wall from the other side. Its heads slowly fades in with its pallor and purple face.

"Oh my God," says I. "Finn?" It is Finn! The frostbite only makes clear sense to me. His face looks so lost, so hopeless.

"Liam," Finn says. "I'm lost."

"Lost?"

"I don't know where I am, Liam."

"No . . . no, this can't be real."

"No, Liam! Please! I don't know where I am!"

"How are you still alive?"

"What?"

"You died, Finn! You drowned yourself in that lake! You gave up on yourself! You gave up on me!"

"What are you talking about, Liam?"

"Oh my God. I'm going fucking crazy!"

"Liam! Please! Please, please, please, please, please, just get me out of here!"

"How? There's a fricken concrete wall between us. How can I even see you?"

"Kill me! Just kill me, Liam! Please! I don't want to be here!"

"What?"

"You need to kill me!"

"I'm going to get you out of there."

"No! You need to kill me!"

"Damn it! I'm not letting you go, Finn! I should've been with you that night. You sat by me on that bus, I knew how you were feeling, I should have been there with you." I kneel by the wall and place my head against it to let gravity take my tears to the drain.

"Liam. You can't blame yourself. We were both depressed that night."

"But coach abused you! I should have said something. I should have told the school and he should've been fired and arrested, and you could still be alive! Everything could still be normal, and we could be playing hockey together."

"Liam. You need to let go of the past. You need to start living in the present and accept what has happened."

"I will never accept what happened! Never!"

"Then don't blame yourself! You know, sometimes, it takes a team. It takes a team to win, it takes a team to lose, and it takes a team to have each other's back."

"But no one was there for you."

"But you were, Liam. You were there for me, always! I just couldn't bare another second." Finn places his hand up on the wall again. "Hey." I look up into his eyes, his ghostly wolf eyes. I take my hand and set it against his. Even though he appears as a ghost, I can feel warmth between us. When I look at our hands together, I see thick, veiny cords attached to his hand. They pulsate like the rhythm of a heart. The cords seem slimy, bloody of course, almost like he's connected to some sort of life support. The cords suddenly yank back from the darkness. Something huffs from the deep.

Finn looks behind him, then back at me. "Put me back where I belong."

Finn's hand rips off the concrete wall as he's pulled into the darkness. I scream for help at the top of my lungs, but it's no help when your voice is naturally deeper than others. I squeeze my hand into a fist and pound on the metal cage.

I'm helpless.

THE MOP

Chester and Ash walk through the double set of french doors and into The Barn. The presence of a baked pretzel roams around the concession area. The door is open to the concessions, the lights are on inside, and a couple of voices mutter through the concession stand's steel gate.

Chester knocks on the open door. Ben sits on the countertop while Danny leans against the counter by the coffee machine. They spin around to discover Chester in the room.

"Hey," Danny says. "Why are you guys here so early?"

Chester moves into the room as Ash follows from behind.

"Ash and I were gonna ask Liam to hang out at my place and play some Chel, but his mom said that he came here to skate a little bit."

"Well," Danny says. "That's weird."

"What?"

"I haven't seen him. Did you see him on your way in, Ben?"

"No," Ben says.

Chester glances at Ash, and Ash throws the glance right back.

"Huh," Chester says. "Oh! Maybe he's on the outdoor ice. We should go check it out." Chester and Ash pivot their bodies towards the warming area.

"No!" Danny says. Chester and Ash stop. "I mean, he can't use that ice anyways. It's covered with snow from the storm. There's no way he's out there."

"It's probably coated in snow like how he eats his butter noodles from Olive Garden," Ash says. "Loaded with parmesan."

"So true," Chester says.

"Plus, it's fricken freezing outside," Ben says.

"Well, have you been around the rink lately?" Chester says. "He probably just snuck into the locker room without you noticing."

"No," Danny says. "I went to the locker room to grab my skates not too long ago. I swear, I haven't seen him."

"That's so weird."

"What?" Ben says.

"Well," Chester says. "Liam's car is outside. I don't know where else he'd be."

"Yeah," Ash says. "It's not normal of him to run away or anything. And it's not like there's anything else nearby the rink that's worth goin to."

"He'll for sure show up around practice time, which is in about two hours," Ben says. "He's not the type to miss practices."

"Well, will you look at that," Ash says, speaking to Chester.

"Someone's a little salty."

"Excuse me?" Ben says. "What the hell did you just say?"

"You heard me. You're intimidated by Liam, aren't ya?"

"Bullshit."

"I bet you can't even list a few good things about Liam."

"BET!"

"Do it!"

"Liam's a hard worker."

"How so?"

"He works hard in practice. He works hard in the gym. But it feels like he's only doing it to make coach happy."

Chester takes over, "Or maybe it's because he fucking loves hockey with all his might and he wants to go far with it in life. Maybe it's because he wants to succeed at something and reach a dream like the rest of us. He wants to push himself to the limit to reach that state tournament he's always dreamt about. Maybe it's because he wants to make the best fucking memories of his high school career his senior year. Maybe it's because he wants to impress his father who died by sliding into the front of a fucking combine! Do you not understand that Liam has had one miserable life and wants to finally do something that makes him stand out? Besides, you're the ones who are here for the show. You're doing this for your egos. You guys don't even believe we can make it to the state tournament. All you believe in is miracles, but miracles are only granted by pure dedication and hard work!" Chester takes a few breaths. "We won't ever stand a chance in sections with your guys' attitude."

Ben's mouth clenches up in fury. Danny dead-on stares at Chester.

Chester directs Ash out the door. When they walk out into the front warming area, Ben slams the door shut from behind them. Ash starts for the long hallway, but as Chester follows, he notices something in the Library of Skates. Something sits under the stray chair in the back corner. He looks back to the concession stand door, which is sealed shut, then he makes his move into the room. He bends down to look at it. It's Liam's sweatshirt and beanie hat.

Chester takes the beanie hat, exits the room, and hustles to the long hallway. The caged lights are still, and the heat feels cozy. He sees Ash halfway to the locker room. He runs down the hall and catches up with him. They walk inside the locker room and sit right next to each other in their stalls.

"Ash," Chester says. "Look."

Ash takes Liam's beanie hat. "Where did you find it?"

"In the sharpening room."

"Do you think Danny has something to do with this?"

"I don't know. I just don't understand where Liam would be right now. It's just . . . I can't bear to think if . . . ."

"I know."

"Maybe we're just freaking out about this. Maybe we should just go on the ice and hope that Liam shows up for practice."

"Yeah."

Chester slides on his compressors. He straps on his crusty knee pads which have dried out from the Dorcha game. Then, he pulls on his white practice socks and tightens his breezers. He grabs his skates from the top hanging racks and shoves his feet inside of them. The ends of the laces are quite rough while the plastic doesn't seem to be holding on to them any longer, but he manages to slide them through the lace holes and tie his skates. He throws his chest pad over his head, then tightly straps the shoulder pads and the two low velcro strips. After he puts the elbow pads on, he pulls on his white practice jersey and reaches for his helmet and gloves from the top of his stall. He sets them down on top of his cubby.

Ash starts lacing his skates when Chester straps on his helmet.

"I'll meet ya out there," Chester says.

"Okay, speed demon," Ash says.

Chester slides his gloves on. As he walks over to the stick stand, his blades click against the rubber. He pulls out his stick from the stand like a sword pulled out from its sheath.

"Oh," Chester says. "Pucks."

"Buckets over here," Ash says. "Behind the stick stand."

"Sweet."

Chester lifts the hefty bucket of pucks and attempts not to stumble his way out the door. He walks down the remainder of the long hallway to the game doors that lead out to the rink. He walks along the rubber path, passing the edge of the student section area. The door to the ice is shut. He places the bucket of pucks down on the concrete by the rubber padding. The door contains a steel lever that needs to be pushed on to open. Chester gives it a shove, but it's stuck. He pushes down harder this time, but nothing. He

182

decides to put all his weight on it, but he ends up lifting his skates off the ground and the handle goes nowhere. He takes the end of his stick and pounds the lever down with a loud clang. Ice shards dart at his face. Now, he pushes down the steel lever and opens the door to the ice.

Before he jumps on, he grabs a few pucks and tosses them onto the ice. He steps onto the ice and closes the door behind him. He takes a step towards the pucks, but his ankle twists to ninety degrees with a crunch. Chester slams his face mask into the ice and wails out a scream. Saliva drips out from his lips and dangles off the edge of his face mask.

He rolls over onto his back. He cries out the pain while looking at the rusted ceiling supports of The Barn. He looks down at his foot. His right foot is bent out of place, over ninety degrees to the right. The toes can almost point at his own eyes. But he notices something at the bottom of his skates: someone stuck sock tape to the bottom of his blades. "Ash!"

As I stand in the zamboni cellar in the dim light, I can hear Chester's yelling through the steel zamboni door. "Chester! Chester, I'm in here!"

"Liam?" Chester says.

"Yes! It's me! I'm in here! Help me get out!"

Chester howls out another scream. "I can't!"

"What!"

The clicking of a metal chain disturbs my attention. The chain to the zamboni door suddenly moves like someone is pulling on it, but there's no one in here but me. The steel door begins to open, higher and higher the door goes. I grasp my fingers around the metal cage as I try to peer over to the ice. I can barely see the top of Chester's body; he's along the near blue line.

"Chester!" says I. He screams in shock. I don't think he's hearing me anymore.

A spark flares down near my face. The roar of an engine burns on. With one click of the clutch, the zamboni rolls in reverse and towards the ice. The dim light shines above me as the zamboni hops its back tires, then its front tires, onto the ice.

"Chester! Get off the ice!" Chester doesn't hear my yelling, but he hears the sound of the zamboni, rolling towards him closer and closer. The zamboni accelerates in reverse, aiming for Chester. "Chester!" He rolls over on his knees and tries to get up. He boosts up on his good foot, but he slips back down onto the ice, landing on his twisted foot. He forgot about the sock tape that still sticks to his blades. The zamboni is near the blue line. He crawls away from it and towards the boards.

Something's putting weight on his foot. The zamboni's back left tire crushes his broken right foot. The tire goes up the back of his legs, crushing the bone against the ice as Chester blares out his scream. The zamboni rolls up to his spine and crackles it with all the weight pressuring against him. Blood blows out from his mouth as I watch it splatter on the white boards.

"CHESTER!"

The zamboni stops while on Chester's back. It squeals its back wheel on his back. Skin rips off from his body while blood splats along the glass. The zamboni moves forward and off of his body, but then moves backwards and over his body again. So much blood floods the surface of the ice.

The zamboni lets down its mop, turns on the water, and moves forward towards Chester. The mop picks up his body and it begins to resurface the ice, starting along the boards. Chester's blood floods all over the surface as more and more comes out from him. The zamboni ovulates around the boards as I watch from the torture of this dark cellar.

A door bangs shut. I look over by the student section. Ash walks up to the edge of the ice. He looks at the bloody ice, confused.

"Ash!" says I. "Ash! Over here!" Ash looks over in my direction. He can't see me. I poke my fingers out through the cage. "Ash! In the zamboni room!"

"Liam?" Ash says. He looks back at the zamboni and watches it pass by with its second ovulation around the rink. Then, he sees a body under the mop. "Oh my God." Ash catches himself from falling to the ground by grasping onto the door. I can hear him puking.

"Ash!" says I. "For God's sake, let me out of here!"

After a few seconds, Ash regenerates himself. He drops down to the rubber platform and unties his skates. He pulls them off and heads over to me in the rest of his gear. The zamboni drives down the center of the ice, the blood still flooding out of his body.

"What the fuck, Liam!" Ash says. "What's going on!"

"Ben and Danny locked me in here," says I. "They locked me in here, and then Chester was hurt or something. The zamboni started to move and . . ." I just happen to realize something happened in that moment. Chester's dead. My best friend, my teammate, my brother, dead. He just died in front of me and I couldn't do anything. I just watched. All I could do was watch.

"I'm going to get you out," Ash says. He searches for the drill on the tool shelf. He finds the hefty drill and looks for the corner bolts, which aren't tough to find. The zamboni rolls around again. It has a couple more ovulations till it has resurfaced the ice with all of Chester's blood.

Suddenly, I hear stomps inside of the rink.

"Who is that, Ash?" says I.

Ash looks over to the bleachers. "It's Danny."

Ash works on one of the bolts with a thick drill bit.

Danny pops in. "What the hell did you do?"

"No!" says I. "What the hell did you do?"

"What?"

"Go take a look for yourself!"

Danny approaches the zamboni doors to the ice, but halts as he watches the zamboni loop around for its last lap. No ones in the driver's seat. He amuses it with frozen shock.

Ash unbolts the first corner. He moves onto the second one.

"Hurry, Ash!" says I.

"I'm trying," Ash says.

The zamboni makes its last turn at the other end of the ice. It's rolling towards the zamboni room. It's rolling towards Danny.

"Danny!" says I. "Get out of its way!" He doesn't barge.

The zamboni rolls over the near blue line. Ash pops out the

second bolt and sets the drill down. He hustles over to Danny and pulls him off to the side. The zamboni finishes a bloody resurfacing and hops its front tires, then back tires, down on the concrete. It rolls over me, and Chester's deformed body pulls in from under the mop. I glance for a second at his bloody face, a few intestines dangle out from his mouth. I duck and cover my head from the sight. The horrid stench of flesh drifts down to me like the inside of a butcher shop. The stench is so strong that I can taste the blood seeping between my teeth and soaking my tongue like water to a sponge.

I curl up into a ball and weep in the darkness.

THE HOCKEY NET

Danny hops on the zamboni, pulling it out from the garage and leaving back Chester's deflated body over my head. Ash embraces the bloody flesh and unbolts the last two corners of the cage. He pulls me out of the cellar. The mixture of blood and oil didn't go with me too well, but my burnt feet distract me from the toxic air. Ben runs over to Danny and stares out onto the ice, shocked by all the blood that freezes into it. Ash pushes the cage back over the cellar so Danny can drive the zamboni back over Chester's body. No one's gonna touch him.

"Jesus Christ," Ash says. "What happened to your feet?"

The thick mucky air of a butcher shop gets to me. While the puke pumps up my throat, Ash keeps me up on my feet and walks me out of the zamboni room.

"Where are you going?" Danny says.

"He needs to sit," Ash says.

Danny moves closer to Ben, watching Ash limp me over to

the game doors and into the long hallway. "Come on, Ben." Danny places his hand on Ben's shoulder. He spins his head around to him. They follow Ash and I down the hallway and into the locker room.

Ash places me in my stall as I plop down and hit my head along the backside wood.

"Imma get you some water," Ash says. He finds the water bottle carrier on the floor and pulls one out. He rushes over to the sink and begins to fill it.

Ben enters the locker room. It's like he's lost in a foreign country or something. Danny helps direct him to his stall. They sit down in their spots across from me. Ben looks down at the floor while Danny is beside him, trying to gain his attention back, but as Danny tries, Ben tilts his head up and locks his eyes on me, not with anger, but fear.

The rusty faucet squeaks off. Ash brings the water bottle to me. I squeeze the bottle, ejecting a jet fume of water into my mouth. Ash looks over at Ben and Danny. Ben takes his eyes back to the floor, but Danny feels his glare.

"What the hell happened?" Ash says. "You guys better start talkin before the other guys get here for practice."

"I don't know," Danny says.

"The fuck you do!"

"I don't know."

"Why did you lie to me about Liam then? Why was he locked in a fricken cellar?"

"Because of his feet."

189

"What about his feet?"

"They were burned." His voice breaks into fragments. "I baked his skates and . . . they just burned." He whispers to himself, "I don't know how."

"Is that true, Liam?" Ash says.

I tighten my jaw and stare dead on into Danny's soul. Everything else around the locker room blurrifies. "Why don't you tell him the truth?"

Danny plays with his fingers, looking down at the floor. "Me, Cole, and Ben, after the Scythes game, pulled Finn aside and . . . We beat him up. We kicked him, we punched him, and he bled all over and--" Ben's snot glides down from his nose as it goops down onto the floor.

Ben wipes the snot away, then sniffles. "We killed him."

"No, we didn't, Ben," Danny says. "We didn't kill him."

"Yes, we did."

"No, we did not."

"We killed him!" Ben drops his head on Danny's chest. Danny gives him a bear hug, holding his head tightly against his shoulder.

Ash seems to have flashbacks of Finn, as so do I.

"I encountered Finn in the cellar." Their attention draws to the sound of my voice.

"What?" Danny says.

"I was in the cellar. You know, the one you locked me in. A while after you guys left me to lone in the dark, I saw Finn. I don't know if I was seeing things or going crazy or what, but I saw him.

His fingers were all frostbitten, his face paler than a ghost, and then he had these cords or tubes connected to the back of his hand, and he said something to me . . . He kept saying to me over and over, 'Put me back where I belong.'"

"You saw Finn?" Ash says.

"Yes. I know how crazy it sounds, but after what we all just experienced, I have no explanation for any of this."

Ben wipes his face with his hands, then looks up at me. "So, what do we do?"

"Well, after everything that I've seen, let's see: First, it was the encounter in my hallway at home. There flooded the hallway with redwater, outside the locker room here, like it was the sinking ship of the Titanic. Then, on the bus ride home, there was a kid standing in front of our bus, but no one else saw it. The blood outside, Finn's blood, it boiled down into the ice and the cold ground. Lastly, there were my skates, burning my skin and blood away, and now it got Chester." I stand up and leap over to the stick stand where a white board leans against it on the floor. I grab the expo marker by the board and draw a visual of The Barn from a worm's eye view: blood on the outdoor rink seeps down into the dirt. The indoor ice freezes the blood on the surface. Finn's body is inside the coffin and under center ice. Then, the blood flooding the hallway.

"What are you doing?" Ash says.

"I think The Barn is a sustenance to Finn. I think it's alive."

"You've got to be kidding," Danny says. "That's your answer? That's your explanation for all of this? Yeah, have fun

191

bringing your conspiracy theory up to the cops."

I grasp Danny's shirt and force his face into mine. "I don't think you should talk to me like that after all of what you did. This is the only explanation I got."

"I believe him," Ash says. He hands me my beanie hat. "I'm with Liam on this."

Ben pushes off his cubby. "I'm with Liam too." He turns around and pulls out his jersey which hangs on the back of his stall. He rips the C off it and hands it to me.

"Ben."

"No," he says. "Liam, you deserve it. I always knew you were more of a leader than I am. Everybody knows it."

I don't know what to respond back with.

"So, what's your plan?" Danny says.

"I don't know. Finn said, 'Put me back where I belong.'"

"Back in the lake?" Ash says.

My eyes shoot up to him. "Yes! Yes! We need to get him out and put him back where he belongs, or at least where he thought he belonged."

"We need to drown him again."

"Yes."

"What about all the blood?" Danny says.

"I don't know," says I. "Let's get out there and figure this out."

I lead them out to the long hallway. We push through the game doors and into the rink.

Chester's body sits under the zamboni mop with his bloody

guts hanging out. My teammate is gone. He's been the only brother to me on this team. Who am I going to hug? Who am I going to talk to? He's the only planet that sustains my happiness on this team, but now he's gone. He's fucking gone!

"Liam," Ash says. "Look."

Ash points to the ice. I walk to the open door and look at it. The blood is disappearing on the sides. From all the sides of the rink, the blood sucks in towards the middle of the rink. The blood flows its own stream, and it's finding its way out. The drain is where Finn and his coffin are buried. The blood seeps closer and closer to the center dot. It all flows to the center, and the faceoff circle wrinkles away like water wears down paper. The ice shreds to pieces and leaves a hole in the ground.

A hand grasps the edge of the ice from within the hole. The fingers are frostbitten, and cords connect to the back of the hand. Then the other hand slams on the ice with more cords on the back. Finn's pale face reveals itself as he pulls himself out of the hole. Huge cords connect to his back. He attempts to crawl over to us, but I start to walk onto the ice.

"Liam!" Danny says.

"Come on!" Ash says. He follows me out onto the ice, then Danny, and then Ben.

"Finn?" says I.

"Get me out of here!" Finn says.

"Danny! Do you have a chainsaw, axe, anything?"

"A skate sharpener, but that'll take a while to tear apart."

"There should be an axe somewhere in a fire box."

"I don't know where it is then."

"Go search for it!"

Danny runs off in search for the fire axe. The plastic air ventilation above the ice puffs up like a bike tire. It sounds like a deep huff from the devil. Finn cries while down on the ice. I slide down to him.

"Hey, Finn, it's alright. I'm here, bud."

"Kill me, Liam. Please, just kill me."

"We're going to get these cords off you."

I stand up, grab Finns' arms, and pull him as far as I can away from the hole. The cords jolt to a stop as I slip on the blue line. Someone's holding the cords from the depths. Finn cries out waterfalls.

"Hey," says I. "Remember that time in Bantams when we traveled five hours north; all the way up to Roseau, along the Canada border?" He nods. "That was our last road trip before high school hockey. We knew we had to make the most of our time."

"We all bought those Boa sticks from that one store."

"Yes! And we all went out to eat at that one restaurant in the middle of the forest."

"I also remember it being super fricken cold."

"Just like today, huh?"

He shivers in fear as his waterfalls start to slow down. "I always loved your dad as a coach," he says. "The early morning practices with donuts, the fun drills, all the planned road trips, all those memories . . . I wish things were still like that."

"I do too. But I'm happy with that past! I'm proud of those

memories with you and the boys, and I wouldn't do anything to change it."

Danny kicks a locked storage door open inside the arena.

"Imma go help search," Ash says.

Ben starts to side-shuffle across the ice towards the zamboni room, but Finn yelps out a scream as the cords pull him back. I hang onto him. We slide like a slug towards the hole.

"Ben!" says I. "Help!"

Ben sprints to the zamboni room and looks around. He notices Chester's corpse still under the zamboni mop. He looks at Chester's skates, then a lightbulb flickers on inside of his head. He unties the skates as quickly as possible. One skate off, and then the other. Then he spins around to the tool shelf and finds a bungee cord on the tool counter. He grabs it and runs out with the gear.

Ben crouches down by me and Finn. "Move your hand, Liam," he says. "Imma tie this skate around his left hand, and then the other on his right." He ties the left skate on his hand, wrapping the lace around the heel and double knotting it. He does the exact same thing to his right hand as we are on the brink of sliding into the hole.

Danny runs into the mini hallway; Ash catches up with him, still wearing his hockey gear.

"Where do you think it is?" Ash says.

"I don't know!" Danny says.

"Where do you think it would be?"

"Maybe in the maintenance room. I don't know!"

Danny opens the door to the referee room at the end of the

mini hallway. He looks on the walls for the axe. Nothing.

"If only you had a map of this place," Ash says.

"Wait!" Danny says. "We do!"

"What?"

"There's a map on the wall up front that shows the emergency exits. Maybe it has the axe on there!" Danny heads out of the locker room. He walks towards the front as Ash follows, but Danny stops in his tracks.

"What?" Ash says. "What is it?" Ash moves in front of Danny and looks in front of the concession stand. A wolf stands in place with nacho cheese around its mouth. It shows its teeth and growls at the boys. "Danny?"

"What?"

"Where's the map?"

"Right side wall."

Ash stares at the wolf as he slowly moves to the ride side of Danny. The wolf watches Ash with its mouth presenting the sharp icicles inside. Ash feels the wall with his hands behind his back, keeping his eyes locked on the wolf. He touches something in the shape of a square, and it has a handle inside of it. He runs his finger over the handle where he can feel the bumps of letters. It's a fire alarm. He keeps moving his hand along the wall as he waddles his feet with caution. The wolf continues to stare at Ash with its ice eyes. Ash feels a cold, metal box with the back of his hand. It has a handle on it, and it's quite bulky to be hanging on the wall. It's the AED box. He waddles to the other side of the box and slides his hand along the wall. Nothing. Ash begins to twist his body, facing his chest towards the front doors of The Barn. He unlocks his eyes with the wolf and looks by the fire alarm. The map is right above it.

"Ash," Danny whispers. "Hurry up, please."

Ash takes another glance at the wolf, then he turns to look at the map. He sees the tornado symbol, and then the arrows which point towards the fire exits. The map marks where the AED is, but it doesn't mark where the axe is.

"Danny," Ash says. "It's not here."

"Ash," Danny says. "Don't move."

"What? What's happening?"

"It's moving. It's moving towards you."

Ash's teeth rattle. "How close is it?"

"Just don't move a muscle."

"God damnit, Danny! Tell me!"

"It's a few feet away from you."

"Please do something." Danny moves a foot back.

The wolf jolts its head at Danny. Danny turns as the wolf jumps at him. He sprints into the mini hallway and crashes into Locker Room 1. He slams the door shut as the darkness floods the room. There's no sign of light inside. The door thrashes Danny's head against it as the wolf jumps into it, but he keeps his back against the door.

Ash looks into the mini hallway where the wolf paws at the door, scratching the maroon paint off of it. He spins around and looks for the axe. He runs into the Library of Skates and looks around, but no axe hangs from the wall.

When he exits the Library of Skates, he notices another door on his right. He props it open and flicks the light on. It flickers like lightning as it shines upon the dark, oily furnace. The fire axe hangs on the wall by the light switch. Ash smashes his elbow into the glass and grabs the axe.

Ash exits the furnace room with the axe, but the wolf stands in his way of the mini hallway, staring at him.

Danny backs up from the locker room door. He grabs the handle and gently pulls back on it, but the door won't budge open. He tries to put more muscle into it, but it's locked shut. He feels for the light switch along the wall and presses the sensor's button. The lights turn on. He turns around to find himself standing in the middle of a snowbound forest. He stands on a rubber floormat like he's walked outside of The Barn, but he knows this isn't where he's supposed to be.

Ash moves with caution towards the wolf. It stands there and looks up into Ash's face. Slobber drips out from the wolf's mouth. Ash inches closer and closer to it, only a few more feet away. The wolf takes a step forward, stopping Ash in his path. The wolf takes another step forward. Ash grasps his hands tightly on the axe's wooden handle. The wolf growls its teeth at him. Ash lifts the axe over his head as the wolf sprints at him. The wolf jumps at Ash as he swings the axe down into the wolf's neck. It crashes into Ash and they both collapse to the floor. He gets off the ground and looks at the wolf, watching it bleed out.

Ash picks up the axe and runs over to the mini hallway. He knocks on the door to Locker Room One.

"Danny! You're safe now!" Ash begins to sprint towards the rink.

"WAIT!" Danny says. "I can't get out!"

"What!"

"The door won't open! Please get me out of here!"

"I have to help Liam! I'll be right back!"

"No, Ash! Please!"

"I'll be back! I promise!"

Ash sprints out to the rink. Ben pulls on the bungee cord that wraps around the skates on Finns' hands, keeping me and Finn from sliding down into the hole, but it's not going to hold for long.

Ash runs out onto the ice with an axe in hand.

"Where was it?" Ben says.

"In the furnace room," Ash says. "By the office."

"That's great!" says I. "Now, help us!"

Ash starts swinging the axe at the bloody cords, and Finn releases a scream. He cuts a cord open as blood sprays out from it like an out-of-control hose. He loads up the axe again, closer to Finn's body this time, trying to break more cords at once. With another slash, Finn screams again with blood flying in the air, raining upon us as his body begins to slide into the hole. Danny swings and swings and swings at the smaller cords that connect to his hands. Blood splatters on my face as Finn screams all the pain away.

"Finn," says I. "It's okay. Look me in the eyes. You're going to be okay!" I take out one of the blades from the skates on his hand. I slam the point of the blade into the ice as Ben keeps pulling away on the bungee cord. Ash releases another swing of a warrior and disconnects more cords.

"There's one more cord left!" Ash says.

Ash loads up his next shot. The cord is connected to his back. Suddenly, the cord releases tension. Ash freezes up. I pull Finn up and onto the ice.

"What happened?" Ben says.

Finn wraps his arms around me in a tight squeeze. The cord yanks us down into the hole.

Splash! I land in sub-freezing water.

The water from the splash rises and instantly freezes over the rink's ice, almost like nothing ever happened. Blood covers the ice around the faceoff dot.

The bubbles from the water fizz around my ears, tickling them. I open my eyes and find Finn's body floating in the water with me. The one cord still connects to his back. I swim up to him, take the other skate blade out from his other hand, and saw the cord out. Blood leaks out from the vein like there has been a shark attack. I search for a way out, but ice roofs over me. This place is familiar, oddly familiar. When I look down towards the bottom of the lake, I notice a hockey net on the sandy floor. I'm in Cedar Lake.

My oxygen flushes out from my airbags. I swim Finn's body down as fast as I can. I propel my feet like an Olympic swimmer, but it's hard not using my arms. I kick and kick and kick till I brush up against sand. I let go of Finn's body at the bottom and step on him with my foot. He's unconscious, and hopefully, he's done with his suffering. I lift the hockey net off the ground and trap Finn inside of it.

I place my feet in the mucky sand and push off with all my power. My head feels light, and I can feel my bones bruising up. The opening should be somewhere nearby. My head bangs against the ice. I'm near the surface. I pound my hand against the ice and swim in search for oxygen. I pound and I pound and I pound. Nothing! Absolutely nothing but ice! My lungs are out of oxygen, my heartbeat is slowing down. I just keep pounding and pounding on the ice, but the sound gets softer as I go.

I can see my father through the ice. He's skating on it with his coaching helmet on. He's showing us a game; Gretzky. Then, I see me and the boys, kneeling to the side. Jake and Charlie are chit chatting side by side, joking about something. Danny taps his stick against Finn's helmet, just his random self doing annoying crap. Ben focuses on the drill, and Ash whispers something to me and Chester, but we can't hear what he's saying. He ends up chuckling anyway. Cole and Thomas look like total goofs, as goalies traditionally are goofy.

Smack! I pound my fist through a thin sheet of ice and prop my mouth open above water. The sun blinds my eyes and the harsh bitter winds smack against my skin. The water feels lukewarm compared to the air. I don't want to get out, but I know I have to. I pull myself up but the thin ice breaks again. I paddle the thin ice off until I hit a thicker patch. Finally, I pull myself out of the water and crawl on my elbows. The water on my body turns into crystals. I can't feel my nose, lips, ears, fingers, or toes.

There's an icehouse about fifty feet ahead of me in the middle of the lake. It's a closer hike than to the shoreline. Finn walked a really long way to get out here.

I scurry as fast as I can with my frozen legs to the icehouse. It's a bland looking icehouse made of white metal and has a blue wooden door. I knock on the door, but no way in hell am I waiting. I twist the knob of the fish house. Locked. I take a step back and load a little bit of warmth into my leg. I kick the door, but my leg is too weak. I load up again, and this time, I release a dampened battle yell and kick the door open, breaking some wood along with it. I move inside and close the door.

A heater sits in the corner near a fishing hole. I crank the propane tank on as the metal clicks and turns red, just like an oven. There's a small kitchen counter with cabinets and a light. I turn on the light inside. Two bunk beds sit at the end of the icehouse. I take the blankets and wrap them around me. Then, I snuggle myself in the bottom bunk, hoping that the heater can bring some life back into me.

STRANDED

Ash crawls over the faceoff dot in his hockey gear where the hole just covered itself up in ice. The axe on the ground drips a bloody mess. The air filtration shuts off and deflates above them. Ben watches Ash on the ground in shock.

"Where are they?" Ben says.

"They're gone!" Ash says. He bends down to his knees on the center dot.

"What? I thought we had them!"

"I don't know what to do!" Ash says, crying his eyes out.

"We'll figure it out!" Ben says.

"No, we won't!"

"Yes, we will!"

"They're dead! They're fucking dead!"

Ben kneels down to Ash and grabs his helmet, facing it towards him. "Hey! We don't know that!" Ash looks down at the ice. "Look at me. Look at me, Ash!" Ash draws his eyes up to

Ben. "We're going to be okay! I promise you!"

A scream echoes into the rink, "Help me!" Ben jolts his head around as Ash ducks his head into his knees.

"Oh my God!" Ben says. He grabs the axe and runs off.

"Wait!" Ash says. "Don't leave me here alone!" Ash shuffles after him. Ben walks to the mini hallway as Ash follows behind, walking on the rubber padding. A loud knocking comes from Locker Room One.

"Danny?" Ben says.

"Ben!" Danny says. "Get me out of here!"

Ben pushes the door open. Him and Ash find Danny up in an oak tree while a grizzly bear stands from under him.

"What the fuck," Ben says.

"Danny!" Ash says. "Can you make a run for it?"

"How!" Danny says. "I'm trapped!"

Ash looks to Ben. "Keep the door open."

"Why?"

"Just do it!"

Ash sprints to the concession stand. He grabs a plastic coffee cup with his hockey gloves and fills it up with nacho cheese. Once it fills up to the brim, he runs back to the locker room and into the snowbound forest.

"Wait!" Ben says. "I'll do it."

"Why?" Ash says.

"It'll be faster without gear on." Ben leaves the door as it begins to swing shut.

"THE DOOR!" Danny says.

Ash sprints to the door and slams his helmet into it. He stops the door in time and keeps it open. The bear turns around and looks at Ben, sniffing its wet nose in the air. Ben takes the coffee cup of cheese and whips it into the forest. The bear moans and sprints towards the cheese. Danny jumps from the tree and plummets into the snow. Ben runs over to Danny and helps him up. They run back to the mini hallway as Ash flushes the door shut from behind them. They all fall against the hallway wall and sit.

"Jesus Christ," Ash says. "What was that?"

"I don't know," Danny says. "Maybe that's where the wolf came from."

"What?" Ben says.

"The wolf. It was in the lobby."

"Yeah," Ash says. "I killed it with the axe!"

"What are you talking about?" Ben says.

"There was a wolf in here when we were looking for the axe!" Ash stands and points down to the concession area. "Look for yourself!" When Ash looks, he notices the wolf isn't there.

Ben stands up and looks with Ash. "Where?"

"It was right there."

"What do you mean?"

"I killed it there. That's where it bled out. I don't understand."

"Geezes, guys!" Danny says. "What time is it?"

"Oh fuck!" Ben says. "Practice is in an hour."

"What are we going to do?"

"We need to do something with the blood."

"And how bout Chester's body?" Ash says.

"I don't know," Ben says. "We're screwed." He slumps down along the wall and slides to the floor. He stares at the fire axe on the floor, watching the blood dry upon the handle. "Wait. I got an idea."

"What?" Danny says.

"Do you have backup fuel for the zamboni?"

Danny marches them down to the zamboni room. He pulls out two gallons of fuel in their red canisters. "We have flammable fluid one, and flammable fluid two. Which one do you guys want?"

"Guys," Ash says. "What if Liam and Finn are under the ice, under The Barn?"

"Ash," Ben says. "We don't have a choice."

"I don't know about this, guys."

"Ben," Danny says. "Help me tear this wood off the wall." Danny and Ben rip the wood off the wall from the tool stand. A hammer and some screwdrivers clang on the concrete floor while slipping from their hooks. Danny slides the wood under the zamboni. Oil drips from the zamboni and puddles on the wood. "Alright. Let's burn this barn!"

"Guys," Ash says. He stares towards the front of The Barn.

"What?" Ben says. Coach Kipp walks in through the double set of french doors. "Fuck! Ash, go distract him."

"What? Why me?"

"Danny and I need to start this fire."

"While he's here?"

"We'll be fast! Go stall him!"

"But—"

"Now!"

Ash finds his skates by the rink's door where he left them and slides them on. He clicks his skates to the long hallway. When he walks through the game doors, he sees Coach Kipp walking down past their locker room. He's heading to his private locker room down its mini hallway.

"Who's that?" coach says.

"It's Ash."

"Ah. How are you?"

"Good."

Coach disappears around the corner of his mini hallway. Ash walks down to it.

Coach types in the passcode on the door-lock to his locker room. A triple beep indicates the correct code. When he unlocks the door and opens it, he finds the clicking of Ash's skates approaching from behind. "Are any of the other boys here?"

"Ugh, just Danny. He's working his shift." Coach chuckles. "Do you mind if I come in?"

"Why? What's up?"

"I need to speak to you about something."

Coach Kipp checks Ash's gear out, bottom to top. "Come in. Let's talk."

Ash clicks his skates into his locker room. A couple of stalls sit in the corner on the left. A shelf with trophies and team photographs sits along the right wall. A clock hangs on the back wall, a few hockey stalls stand to the left of the clock. Ash takes a seat in another stall that sits across from the other ones. It's empty, but the top shelf holds a few folded towels. Coach Kipp sits in his stall across from Ash.

"What do you want to do in practice today?" coach says.

"I'm not sure. We could probably work on offensive zone."

"And what makes you think that?"

"Our last game versus Dorcha. We could have scored more goals, but some of the guys need to learn how to pass the puck."

"Yes. I agree we have a few puck hogs."

"That's actually what I wanted to talk about."

"What do you mean?"

"Well, I don't understand why you don't play me. I'm always sitting on the bench and watching first line fuck the game up, and it seems to be every fricken game. I'm working out every day in the gym. I give it my all in practice. But I do all of this just to be benched."

"Ash, the guys on first line, especially Ben, they simply rank higher on the board. They have the most goals and assists on the team. If you want to play first line, I need to see more potential in you."

"But you only played first line in the first game of the year! You spoiled them with that chance to have higher points than me. How am I supposed to get points when you barely give me the opportunity?"

"Look, these guys worked their way up to those positions the past years in high school."

"And I didn't? Liam too. We both worked the same amount

of time as Ben and Danny did, and actually, Liam and I are the hardest working guys on this team! Plus, you've never seen a game from our past years in high school. You're a fricken outsider!"

"Yes, I agree you two are very defined workers, but Ben and Danny score higher—"

"Enough with the points, coach!" Coach Kipp shuts his mouth. His eye whites burn red. "Sorry. But when the next big group of kids tryout for this team next year, when most of us will be gone, you won't have points to choose from. You need to make a team based off how hard kids are willing to work. The only teams that'll make it to state are the ones packed with self-driven and determined guys. They're the ones who'll be state-bound."

Coach Kipp studies my face. "I'll tell you what. I am a forgiving man." Ash thinks about rolling his eyes, but he doesn't. "Maybe we can make a deal out of this."

"What do you mean?"

Coach Kipp moves down to the floor and in front of Ash. "I want you to do something for me. Only a strong man will be capable of doing so though. I don't know if you'll be able to deliver."

"No. I can do it. Just tell me what you want done."

"When we go out for practice, you'll somewhat 'accidently' cripple your best liney."

"What?"

He places a hand on Ash's thigh. "No one will know about this conversation we had. I can give you more playing time if you give me a little something back. Maybe you can even be the line starter for the rest of the year. But I don't know if you have the strength to do it." Ash doesn't respond. He closes his eyes shut. Coach Kipp takes his hand and clenches his fingers around his face mask. "Answer me! You want more playing time? Well, you'll hurt Liam for me. He doesn't seem to care about me. Why should I feel to care for him? Hm? I don't understand who raised that kid, but he sure has one fucking arrogant attitude."

"So, you're asking me to hurt him?"

"I'm asking you if you have the strength. If you can't help me, I guess you'll just have to sit on the bench and fill up water bottles for the team like your wimpy panzy friend."

Ash kicks coach in the gut with the toe of his skate. He darts it for the door, but it's locked. He notices the keyhole from the inside, but no keypad. The keypad is only on the outside. He turns around to find Coach Kipp standing up on his feet again.

"You have strength, but you don't have a brain whatsoever. Don't you know I always like to keep my door locked?"

"You're a fucking freak!"

"Oh, I'm a freak?" Coach Kipp takes a leap at Ash and throws a bursting punch into his gut. Ash coughs out spit. Coach throws punches in his gut again, and then a third time. Ash falls against the wall and slides to the floor in the corner.

"Help!" His voice is broken from the pain. "Danny!"

Coach Kipp kicks him in the corner. Ash takes his gloved hands and blocks his helmet. He curls his shin pads up to his chest. When coach stops kicking him, he grabs his jersey and pulls him over to the stall, stretching his jersey collar along the way. He pulls him up and sets him in the stall.

"Take your helmet off," coach says. He begins to unlace Ash's skates. Ash shivers in the stall. Coach pounds his fist into the side of his helmet. "Take it off!" When he unlaces a skate, he rips it from Ash's foot, pulling him from the stall. Coach pushes him back against the stall and helps him unstrap the helmet. He throws the helmet aside in the room as it clangs off the wall and onto the floor. "Lift your arms." Ash lifts his arms and coach pulls his jersey off. Ash is shirtless under his pads. "You aren't wrong when you said you worked out." Ash takes his hands and shoves them at coach's shoulders. He struggles to move from coach's strength.

"Help!" Ash says. "Danny!"

"You're not going anywhere. You'll be a perfect boxing bag in my room."

Ash takes the blade of his other skate and kicks it high at coach's shoulder. The blade slices open his jacket. Coach Kipp yells back from the cut and falls into his stall. Ash puts his weight on Coach Kipp and wrestles for control of his arms. "Where's the key?" Coach Kipp slaps at Ash's hands. "Where's the key!" Coach jumps off his back with all his might, and he pushes Ash with his hands as he goes flying back to the stall, his head slamming into the stall's upper shelf. His chin slams down into his chest, his teeth clatter, and he falls down to the floor. Coach Kipp wipes the blood that leaks out from his shoulder.

Unconscious, Ash loses all signs of hope.

FIREFLIES

Danny spills a trail of gasoline towards the away teams' locker rooms; they're shabby, cold, and dark locker rooms that sit to the right of the zamboni room. He walks backwards by the locker room doors with the numbers of 4 and 3 painted above them in black. At the corner of the rink, where the old high school locker room was located, which is now used for the youth coaches, the path bends with the boards. Danny keeps pouring the fuel along the rubber while walking to the away bench. He hops onto the bench's platform and spills the fuel all over it.

When he reaches the penalty box and scorer's area, he turns back around and continues the line of gasoline behind the benches. A broadcasting box pokes out from the wall and stands above the benches. It looks over the whole arena, right above the scorer's box. Danny walks under the box and continues the line of gasoline.

Danny passes the home bench and encounters the boards

again. He follows the bend past the vintage locker room, which gets taken over by the bantam teams who think they run this place. Just wait till high school kids.

Danny pushes a door open and chains it to the wall with the built-in door holder. He pours the gasoline in the mini hallway. His canister empties as he dumps the rest of it out.

Ben starts at the zamboni room and continues the trail from the ice. He walks up the wooden steps of the bleachers. He dumps the gasoline all along the walking platform by the glass. Once he reaches the end, he jumps up a step and pours the line on the next level. He ducks under the stair rails on the bleachers and keeps moving forth. When the platform ends, he jumps the next and repeats.

Ben finishes the bleachers off at the top of the student section and leaves. He continues the fuel line through the game doors and into the long hallway. The strong gasoline takes a toll on Ben as he places his hand on his head. He blinks his eyes up and down like he has eyelashes in them. He doesn't stop moving though. He passes the coach's locker room, then his locker room, and continues all the way down to the dryland room. His canister empties around the corner of the long hallway and near the Library of Skates.

Danny crosses in front of the double set of french doors from the mini hallway. He encounters Ben and his empty fuel canister in front of the concession stand. Danny grabs his canister and throws them into the furnace room.

"Will this do?" Ben says.

"It'll do," Danny says. "Fire spreads fast."

"Yeah, but most of the hallway is made out of concrete."

"As long as Chester's body burns up, then we can cover ourselves."

"You're right. We should probably move his body on the ice then because he has his gear on, and the blood on the ice right now can be seen as his."

"But no skates."

"Where are we going to get skates? We can't take someone else's."

"Did you spill fuel in the locker room?"

"No, I didn't feel the need to."

"I'll take a pair from the office. No one should notice."

A door slams shut. Jake and Charlie walk into the warming area, giggling. Cole also enters a few steps behind them. Ben and Danny stand shoulder to shoulder.

"What's up, goons," Charlie says.

"Nothing," Danny says.

"Oh, how's that arm doin, Charlie?" Jake says.

"It's healing," Charlie says.

"I'll be right back," Ben says. He stares in Danny's eyes for a second, almost as if he is speaking to him through his mind, then leaves the group.

"Yeah," Cole says. "That guy fricken pounded on it! I saw the whole thing from my net!"

"Wow, I'm happy I can bet on you when I'm in danger," Charlie says. "Nah, it wasn't too bad. My parents didn't want to pay for the stiches, but it's healing. Slowly, but surely."

Ben turns the corner and into the long hallway. He mall walks at first, but he builds up speed to a jog and soon enough, he's sprinting down the long hallway, passing the dryland room, then the locker room, then coach's locker room, then the girls' locker room, and ending at the game doors. He crashes through the doors, then ducks behind the bleachers. He runs over to the boards and stays hidden under the glass. He enters the zamboni room through the door while the gate is wide open, exposing Chester's suited-up, deflated bloody body. He looks around for something that will trigger the fire. Screwdrivers litter the floor, and a couple of hammers are under the shelf. He takes a screwdriver and a hammer, then grinds them together like they're wooden branches from the woods. No sparks emit. He peeks out the doorway and sees Danny still conversing with the guys, but Cole starts to leave the group and towards the long hallway.

Ben squirms through the messy tool shelf. His fingers land on the drill that bolted the cage for the cellar. He sets the hammer in the trail of gasoline, right below the zamboni gate. He plugs the drill in to the nearby outlet, right next to the door. Then, he places the tip of the drill bit onto the hammer. With a pull of a trigger, the drill bit spins onto the hammer while the sparks burst into fireworks. As soon as the sparks flutter onto the fluid, the fire erupts into a wild beast. The trails immediately ignite into flames. Ben watches the fire as it flies onto the ice and races towards the long hallway and passes by the away bench. The fire reaches the bleachers. Ben turns around and hears some sort of crackling. The fire burns on the wood under the zamboni. He sprints out the exterior door of the zamboni room that leads him outside.

He jumps into the snow. The industrial door slams itself shut. Ben stands up onto his feet in the ankle-deep snow. He stares at the zamboni gate from outside. The whistling wind shakes it as it makes the sound of a carabiner hitting against a flagpole. A deep boom rattles the steel gate. Ben leaves and runs around the arena towards the front entrance.

Cole walks into the long hallway and finds liquid shimmering on the ground. He hears a soft roar towards the end of the hallway. Fire streaks through the game doors and down the long hallway towards him. He turns and bolts off towards the front as the fire follows him.

"We need to get out!" Cole says.

"What?" Charlie says.

The guys notice the fire blazing at them.

"Go!" Danny says. He pushes them with his hands to the doors. They run out of there.

Ben comes sprinting around the corner of The Barn and meets them outside in the parking lot.

"Where did you come from?" Jake says.

"Well, I was in the zamboni room," Ben says. "I saw a fire and it was approaching the zamboni. So, I exited out back and came here."

"Are there sprinklers in there?" Cole says.

"Yes," Danny says. "They should turn on automatically."

"Oh my God," Ben says.

"What?" the boys say.

"Did Ash come out?"

"Wait," Cole says. "Ash is in there?"

"Oh no," Danny says. "He's in there with coach."

"We need to go back in there!" Charlie says.

"No!" Danny says. "The firetrucks should be on their way. I can't let you go in there."

"You aren't stopping me." Charlie walks up to the french doors while Danny tries to push him back. An explosion bursts through the front of The Barn, over by the Library of Skates.

"That's the furnace room," Danny says. "Now you're definitely not going inside." Charlie steps back. "Okay. Let's go. We can't stand here. Move!" Danny pushes them away from the rink as Ben stands to the side, looking through the doors. "Ben, come on!" Ben looks back at Danny. "Don't do it, Ben."

Ben hustles through the double french doors and into The burning Barn.

WILDFIRE

The flames from the furnace room burn the white ceiling tiles
away. The lights burst into flames and wave through the filthy
smoke that rivers itself to the front doors. Ben runs across the
room to the gasoline trail. It's burning into the rubber and towards
the walls, but Ben jumps over the trail and lands on the dry rubber.
He sprints down to the start of the long hallway. The flames melt
the rubber by his feet and grow out to the sides. With one deep
inhale, his chest rises, his knees bend, and his mind prepares.

He swings his arms with a jolt and sprints along the wall. He
passes the dryland room as the flames lick his leg hairs. His legs
gallop with the concrete wall like a horse, floating in midair at
times. He reaches the locker room door and smashes it open.

"Ash?" Ben says. "Ash, you in here?"

Ben notices his gear in his stall, drying from the Dorcha
game. He walks over to it and begins to put his gear on. He starts
with his bottoms, then laces his skates on, straps on his top pads,

pulls over his game jersey with a missing C, straps on his helmet, and slides his gloves on.

If Ash and Coach Kipp aren't inside of the locker room, then they must be in coach's room.

When he opens the locker room door, the fire burns to both sides of the wall. He takes a step out with one skate, then the other. He walks through the flames as he feels his skates warming up, almost as if they are being baked. He hurries to the hallway extension of the coach's room. Luckily, he didn't spill gasoline near his door.

Ben walks up to the door and pushes it. Locked. He pounds on it. "Ash? Ash, are you in there?"

"Help!" Ash yells. "Help—" His voice muffles.

"I'm coming, Ash! Back away from the door!"

Ben walks back to the flames. He spins around and bolts at the door. He jump-checks into it and breaks the lock. He flies into the room and lands on the floor. When Ben looks up and around the room, he sees Ash in his compression shorts while Coach Kipp walks towards him. Coach picks Ben up and throws him against the wall. Ben flops down to the floor like a fish dropped on a boat. Coach picks him up again, but Ash jumps onto him from behind and chokes him by locking his arms around his neck. Ben stands back onto his feet and punches coach in the gut. Coach rips Ash's arms off from his chokehold but stumbles into the doorway. Ben sprints his way at coach. He pushes coach out of the locker room and throws him into the fire. Coach's head smashes against the concrete wall. He falls down to the burning floor.

219

"Ash?" Ben says. Ash cries into his hands while sitting on the floor. His abs have reddened. Blood leaks out of his nose and off the side of his lip. Ben walks over, standing over him in his gear, and bear hugs Ash. Ash squeezes his arms around Ben. Ben sees his jersey and pants in the corner of the room. "Hey, put those on quick. We need to leave."

Ash turns around and slides on his sweats. He takes the baggy practice jersey and throws it on. Before he walks out of the room with Ben, he turns around and remembers the beanie hat that he had when it was left behind.

"Ready?" Ben says. Ash nods and finishes his tears.

Ben picks Ash up off of his feet. He carries Ash into the long hallway. He walks over the growing fire of The Barn as it burns the rubber away. Coach's body burns in the background, but Ben only looks forward. Another explosion blasts from behind him. A roar of flames chases them through the long hallway. The caged lights swing from the metal rafters as The Barn tremors in anger. Ben's feet burn inside of his skates, but he's a hockey player. Hockey players can handle anything in their space suits.

Ben turns the corner as the flames almost blow him out of the hall, but he catches himself from dropping Ash. He runs through the french doors and onto the tarred parking lot, his skates scraping against the concrete. The boys all come after him and Ash. Ben sets him down on the ground and rests. He extends his legs out and unlaces his skates.

"Geezes, Ben!" Danny says. "You scared the life out of me!" He hugs Ben in a tight squeeze. Then, he moves to Ash and gives

220

him a hug. "Where's coach?"

Ben drops his head down.

A crunching of rocks grows behind them. They all turn to find Thomas looking at The Barn which burns away in the cold whistling wind.

ABOMINABLE SNOWMAN

The heater finally brings warmth to me in the icehouse. It smells of fish and burning metal inside this small home. My skin burns like soaking in a hot shower after being in the extreme cold. The blood rushes back through my veins, and I can feel it down in my toes and up in my fingertips. I'm trapped here. All the other fish houses are on the other side of the lake, and it's still early for fish houses to even be out here on the ice. I look down into the fish hole where the sunlight illuminates the ice; there's only four feet augured down. This house can technically collapse through the ice at any minute.

A thermometer hangs by the door. I shuffle my way from the bottom bunk and through the kitchen, the blankets still snuggled around me. The thermometer is plastic, white, and decorates with fish and seaweed. The red liquid freezes at the negative thirty mark. It has dropped from this morning's temp. The wind whistles from outside and blows flurries into the side of this tin can.

I can hear something in the background. There's a constant hum of some sort. It's like a hum of an engine, but it didn't seem like a car's engine. Maybe it's a snowblower? The hum gets louder and more noticeable. I open the door to the wind pushing the door back. I sneak through the crevice and shut the door, trapping the heat in. I scurry to the other side of the icehouse where the hum echoes from. Snowmobilers.

"Hey!" I yell. I can't seem to get any power out of my voice. It crackles like Pop Rocks through my throat. "Hey! Over here!" The snowmobilers ride along the country roadside, way out in the distance. They can't see me, nor hear me. I hustle back inside the icehouse, sneaking through the crevice of the door. I drop the heavy blankets to the floor and rummage through the cabinets. There sits a medical kit. I tear it open as I shiver. Nothing but band aids and Neosporin cream. I slide open a drawer and find a steel whistle. I throw the whistle on and hurry outside with a blanket. I blow all my might through the whistle. It carries in the wind. They keep moving in the distance, but I think they're slowing down.

The snowmobilers stop. I can hear their engines dampen to a silence. They stand next to each other and look out onto the lake. I blow and blow my whistle, but they don't move. So, I take my blanket and wave it in the air like a flag. I keep blowing a steady rhythm with the whistle, which feels like it's freezing onto my lips. They run onto their snowmobiles and crank them on. They move forward on the road, but then u-turn and head down the snowy hill. They're speeding across the lake to me. I blow and blow the whistle as they keep coming and coming. They see me. I spit the whistle out, wrap the blanket around me, and fall down to the ice on my knees.

They park their snowmobiles to the side and hustle over to me. A guy and a woman open their wind guards on their helmets.

"Oh my," says the woman. "We need to get him inside." She helps me onto my feet and supports my walk to the icehouse. The guy opens the door in the whirling wind and closes it behind us. She walks me over to the bottom bunk and sits me down. The guy grabs the other blanket on the ground and wraps it around me. "Casey, see if you can make him something hot."

Casey finds a coffee machine under the sink. He sets it on the counter and fills the coffee pot with glacier cold water. Then, he preps it on the heating metal.

"Hey," says the woman. "What's your name?"

"Liam." I hope they can hear me.

"Nice to meet you, Liam. I'm Carlie, and that's Casey." I nod for a hi. "Can you tell us what's wrong? What happened?"

"I . . . fell . . . in the lake."

"Where are your parents?"

"Mom."

"Where's your mom?"

"Home."

"Are you out here with a friend?"

"No."

"You're alone?"

"Yes." I can hear the water bubbling up. Casey finds an open box of hot chocolate in the back of the cabinet.

"I think we should bring you to a hospital."

"No."

"You need to. Your fingers, your face—" She gasps when she looks at my burned feet. "We need to get him to a hospital, Casey. Maybe call for an ambulance or a helicopter."

"No, please . . . Can I have the phone? I want to call a friend."

Carlie unzips here snowmobiling jacket and reaches into a pocket. She pulls out her phone and brings up the dial. She hands it to me.

"Thank . . . you," says I.

She gets up and helps Casey with the cocoa. The phone rings.

"Hello?"

"Ash."

"Liam?"

"Yes, it's me."

"Holy shit! Where the hell are you?"

"On the lake."

"On the lake?" All the boys around Ash are shocked. "Where on the lake?"

"In an icehouse . . . behind Finn's house . . . in the middle of lake."

"Okay, bud. We're on our way! Hang in there!"

Before I hang up, I can hear sirens in the background, but then Ash cuts off. Casey trades me the hot cocoa for the cell phone. He hands it back to Carlie.

"How are ya feeling, sport?" Casey says.

"Like the abominable snowman." They smile at each other.

"Are your friends coming for you?"

"Yes."

"Drink your cocoa then. You got some warming up to do."

THE SLED RIDE

I finish my warm cup of hot cocoa in these cozy blankets. My eyes
want to close but the pain of my feet and the burning of my toes
and fingers won't let me rest. Casey unzips his heavy jacket and
snow pants.

"Liam," Casey says. "Stand up, bud."

"Your friend, Ash," Carlie says. "He texted me back
wondering if you can make it to this Finn's house?"

"Yes. Take me there."

"Here," Casey says. "Let's put these on. They'll keep you
warm on the ride."

Casey puts the jacket on me, pulling the sleeves over my
arms and zipping the jacket up. He puts the helmet on my head
and puts the mask down. Then, he slides the snow pants on for me
while lifting my legs up from the floor.

"Should I take my boots off for him?" Casey says.

"I wouldn't," Carlie says. "It'll hurt his feet more."

"Alright. Then I think we're set. You ready, bud?"

"Yeah."

Casey supports me as Carlie holds the door open for us. She turns off the heater and closes the door of the icehouse. Casey lifts me down to the ice. He hops on the snowmobile, and I get on behind him. Carlie revs hers up and pushes her helmet mask down.

"Where's his house, Liam?" Carlie says. I point to it on the shoreline.

"Hang on tight, Liam!" Casey says. "Whatever you do, don't let go!"

With me giving a thumbs up and wrapping my arms around him, clasping my hands tightly together, he rips off with the snowmobile as we go gliding across the ice. The force pulls me back, but my hands are glued stuck. The flurries whip past my helmet as we go fast on an open freeway of ice and snow. The ride is so smooth, which reminds me of the open hole, but we're going so fast that the snowmobile would just slide over it like nothing. Besides, my voice needs a rest from yelling.

The wind fluffs up the heavy jacket I wear. The cold wind whistles around the helmet. Casey's hair flies in the wind. Carlie drives out in front. The snow from her snowmobile blows to the side with the wind like dust whirling out in the air from a car on a gravel road. The warm thoughts help me through this miserable trip. Oh, how good would it be to be inside of a hot tub right now!

We make it to the shoreline of Finn's house. They climb their snowmobiles up the hilly backyard and to the side of the house. Ash's Jeep awaits on the curbside. Ben, Danny, and Ash all hop out of the car and confront the snowmobiles. Casey helps me off. The guys run through the thick snow for a group hug. They all hug me, then lift me up and take me to the jeep.

"Thank you for your help, guys," Ash says.

"No problem, man," Carlie says.

"We hope you get better, Liam!" Casey says.

"Thank you," says I. "I won't forget you guys."

Ben sits in the back seat with me. Ash shuts the door and buckles up in his driver's seat. He whips the Jeep out onto the road and into farmland. I lay across the leather seats, my head resting upon Ben's leg. I look up at the ceiling as he looks down at me.

"We did it," Ben says. "We killed it. The Barn burned down. Fire trucks rushed in and sprayed down the flames. The foundation of the rink is still there, but we're all safe now."

I move my eyes to Bens' eyes, and a little smile grows on my face.

After driving through the snowy crop fields, Ash finally brings me into our town's hospital. It sits upon a hill, between the church and the cemetery that overlooks the hill and The Barn off in the countryside. They carry me inside the sliding doors of the hospital and call for help. A few nurses pop out from the swinging doors with a rolling medical bed. They lay me down on the white sheets and start working on me. They roll me through the swinging doors as I watch Ben and Ash disappear from behind them.

BONFIRE

The clouds move across the sky so fast but yet so silent. The graveyard fills with the vague sound of the pastor's voice and cries from Chester's parents. I sit upon a bench, sitting off to the side of the others, alone. The boys stand in a group, besides Chester's loved ones, letting their tears fall through the snow and to the frozen dirt beneath them.

Chester's mother steps forward and places a photo of him with his parents inside of the empty casket. She bends down and gives the photo a kiss. She reaches into her jacket and takes out a teddy bear, placing its arms around the photo. His father walks beside his mother, placing Chester's gaming console and controller inside of the casket. His mother yells her voice out into the treetops. Chester's father bends down to her. He hugs her in a tight squeeze as they cry their tears out.

When they step back from the casket, Ash grabs something from Charlie. He takes Chester's jersey, number 19, and walks towards the casket. The jersey sways in the wind as Ash walks closer to it. The boys watch him from behind as he walks alone, letting all the pain drip away. He reaches the casket and looks down into it. He stares at it, then holds the jersey to his face and cries into it. I push myself off the bench and begin to walk. My medical boots flush down into the snow as I make my way to him.

I place my hand on Ash's shoulder. As he continues to cry into his jersey, I take his head and settle it upon my shoulder. I spill my flood out as we both whimper into his empty grave. Chester was our beloved friend, and he's always kept us connected in love. He was my linemate; he was my teammate. He was a teammate who was there for me whenever I needed him most. I wish you were here Chester. What will I do without you? What is life without you?

Ash and I lay the jersey in the casket, facing 19 towards the fast-moving clouds. I drop to the ground on my knees and hide my face with my arms around my head. Ash kneels down and grasps his arms around me. We cry the rest of our tears out to the ending ceremony. We all watch as Chester's beloved casket sinks into the ground.

After the burial, later that night, me and the boys sit around a bonfire perched on a hill in the middle of the woods. The trees make a perfect circle around this area, making it a perfect viewing spot of the frozen lake and the nighttime sky. The stars above twinkle, brilliant and beautiful. Warmer air in the thirties has arrived again. It's a peaceful and relaxing, cozy night in the countryside.

Ash walks over and hands me a s'more.

"Thank you," says I. I take a bite, and it's rich with its gooeyness. The Hershey's chocolate melts to the tongue. Some of the marshmallow sticks to the bottom of my chin. Ash wipes it off with his hand.

"How are your feet doing?" Ash says. He sits down next to me as the heat from the fire warms my face again.

I look down at my feet, which are in their medical boots. "They're healing. Doctors said it may be a month till they start looking normal again."

"It's a good thing they didn't have to cut any of your toes with scissors," Danny says. "Did they believe the story?"

"Yes. My feet were burnt from the fire, and the frostbite was from the cold outside."

While we watch the fire burn, and some of the boys prep for their s'mores, Ash leans into me, wanting to whisper something. "Liam?"

"What's up?" says I.

"Do you really think we killed it?"

"What do you mean?"

"What I'm trying to say is . . . Do you think it died, or did we just cripple it?"

I stare into his eyes, wanting an answer to pry through my lips, but only the fresh air seeps in. "I mean, I'd like to hope so." Ash looks back into the waving flames.

Jake impresses Charlie on the other side of the fire, burning the marshmallow into a torch. The marshmallow melts off the stick and into the fire. They laugh but try to hide it like they're in a full classroom that's trying to take a test.

Thomas and Cole chitchat to one another. What do goalies even talk about anyways? All I know is that they're probably going to start leaping over the fire to see who can't end up burning their clothes off first, or worse, showing their glove and blocker skills to each other.

Danny and Ben sit to my right, and Ash on my left.

"You know what, guys," says I. "For once, I actually feel like a team of brothers. We lost some good guys along the way, but it ended up bringing us together. As funny as it sounds, for as long as we have been playing hockey together, for basically are whole childhood, I don't seem to know much about you guys."

"Like what?" Ben says.

"Your personal lives."

"Well, what do ya want to know?" Jake says.

"Anything you want to talk about."

"I'm going to ask Rachael out to Snowball next weekend," Jake says. Charlie rapidly taps Jake's shoulders with his hands.

"We still have Christmas break to go through, Jake," Danny says.

"You got a point!"

"I got accepted into my college last night!" Thomas says.

"And I have officially decided to join the Army," Ash says.

"I got an invitation from a college hockey league for tryouts next summer!" Cole says.

"Geezes," says I. "You guys actually have a life outside of

hockey?" We laugh around the burning wood, but something heavy settles in Ben's mind. "How bout you, Ben? What's on your mind right now?"

He picks at his fingernails. "My parents are going to kick me out of the house soon."

"What?" Cole says.

"I rejected Harvard."

"You got accepted?" Danny says.

"Yes, but I rejected it in front of my parents and . . ." He faces his head down to the melting snow.

I walk in front of him and speak to him, one on one. "Ben, look at me." I raise his chin with my fingers. "Look at me. First of all, fuck your parents. Their decision and opinions shouldn't dissolve into yours. You're just a sponge soaking up all their crap that they settle on the table. Don't take it. Not all of them are going to understand what our beliefs are or what we live through on a daily basis. But most importantly, if your parents kick you out of the house for certain, you should always know there's an empty room in my house open for you, always!"

"Same here," Danny says.

"Thank you, guys," Ben says.

"Oh, Liam," Ash says. "Before I forget . . ." He reaches into his sweatshirt pouch and pulls out my beanie hat. "Catch." I snug the beanie hat over my head.

"Thanks, Ash," says I. "Where did you find it?"

"In The Barn, you know, when all that, stuff, happened."

I smirk at him. "And speaking of The Barn, I wanted to bring you all some good news to the bonfire tonight. The Barn is starting its renovations. The rink will be the same layout, but our locker room has doubled in size."

"No way!" Charlie says. "How so?"

"Well, I was told there would be more stalls with the new additions coming up next year, and it would be expanded in size to fit stalls in the center of the room, like it's an island of a kitchen. And there'll be a tv in there for video games!"

"Oh fuck yeah!" Ash says. "I'm bringing my console!"

"Bring Chel too!" Jake says.

"Hell yeah!" Charlie says. They high-five each other.

"The Barn should be complete in a few of weeks, but we have practice scheduled next week at Le Seuers' sketchy Hockey Box."

"Wait," Ben says. "I thought we were done with hockey."

"Yeah," Thomas says. "We don't have enough guys to play."

"Nor a coach," Danny says.

"Actually, we gained some recruits. There are a few boys over in Prior Lake, sophomores in high school, who didn't make it to varsity, and our school is allowing some of them to join up with our team."

"But who's our coach, Liam?" Jake says. I look over at Ash, and we smile at each other. Then we look back to the group. "Who is it?"

"My mom," says I. They all jump and cheer from their seats.

"No fricken way!" Danny says. "I love Jenny!"

"And while I had to spend some time in the hospital, Ash and

I created something for you guys." Ash takes out his sling bag and reaches inside. He grabs something on the inside and pulls it out. It's a long-sleeved shirt. The shirt is in a black and white design with our logo out front, and on the back, it reads *the team of brothers.* "I know, it's a little cheesy but—" We pass them out to the guys, and they put them on. "Once a team, always a team."

"These are sick, dude!" Charlie says.

"Yeah, these are pretty epic!" Cole says.

I look at their shining smiles, but then I realize I need to tell them one more thing. "Guys. I'm sorry, I forgot to mention this. Yes, we can still play hockey. Yes, we gained new recruits for our team. But we can't compete in playoffs. We can't play in state." Ben and Cole look down. Ash watches them with me.

"Well then what's the fucking point of playing then!" Danny says.

"Jesus Christ, Danny," Ash says.

"Ash!" says I.

"What? I'm sick and tired of his attitude!"

"Shut the fuck up, Ash!" Ben says.

"Don't tell me to shut the fuck up!"

"GUYS!" Cole says. "STOP!" Cole faces me. "Liam, why can't we go to state?"

"We're already in motion for the season. We had two games under our belt, and the state doesn't think it's fair to the other teams that we're adding new players and gaining a new head coach with all of this."

"Not fair?" Ben says. "I'll tell you what's not fair! The

Huskies get to stay single A no matter how many times they get to go to state!"

"Well," Thomas says. "They are good."

"They're only good because they live in the North."

"That's not true," says I.

"Okay, Liam," Ben says. "You tell me why they're good then? Huh? Why is their team making it to state every year?"

"They have a team! They have a team of players who actually support one another! I bet they all go to the outdoor rink on every school night to bond with each other. I bet they don't have lazy asses on that team that want to sit at home and do nothing. All I know is that our team has no hope. We don't have a leader. We don't have a ton of players who want to work towards their goals. All we have are a bunch of ego-hunting boys who lie to themselves. They lie to themselves about how 'we're going to have a great season this year!' Look where we're sitting! My fucking friends are dead! Finn and Chester are gone forever!" Everyone sits in silence around the crackling fire.

"And what about you, Liam?" Ben says.

"What about me?"

"Do you think you're a leader? Do you think you're a leader in anybody's eyes? Because all I know is that you sit out when we want to do something. You decide to stay home. You're an introvert, Liam."

"Well, have you ever thought why I don't hang out with you? And honestly, no one else bothers me besides you, Ben. While you had that C on your jersey, you picked your favorites on the team, and you made the ones you liked feel accepted. I never felt accepted! You've always treated me like a child! You think you stand in a bigger position with that C on your jersey but let me tell you something. You ripped that C off your jersey and handed it to me. That shows me you did see something inside of me. You saw something strong inside of me. So, when you ask me if I think I'm a leader, well, I'm definitely starting to feel like one, and that's only because someone told me so." I take out the C inside of my pocket and throw it into the fire. Ben watches it as it burns into ashes.

We sit around the campfire for the rest of the starry night. The last of the flames burn into the dawn, waving the bruises goodbye. Our team will never forget the past as it'll always cherish as memories. We are a constellation and will be remembered when people look up to that starry night. In my eyes, we didn't win as a team. We suffered as a whole, but we will never forget the burns that we left behind.

Penalties were committed, but I hope we learn from them.

END OF BOOK ONE

Writer's Note

After high school, I blasted off to writing school down in Florida. I moved from Minnesota and left all of my family and friends to chase a dream. While I was down in Florida for a couple of months, homesickness crashed into me like a freight train. I didn't just miss my family, but I knew something else was missing from my life. I began to evaluate my life and tried to figure out was wrong. When November hit, I realized that hockey season was sparking up back home. This is the first year that hockey was taken out of my life (excluding the time I had shingles and skipped a year). I wanted to play again so bad, or at least I wanted to be back home to support my team and watch high school hockey again. My school didn't have any athletic sports, and the nearest hockey rink was a thirty-minute drive. I didn't have a car, I barely had any available friends during this time, and my bike broke. I brought my skates down to school to hopefully skate a lot, but that never happened. While I was quarantined in my apartment for months, and this was before the Corona Pandemic hit, I ended up stressing out so much about my dream that I ended up writing my hockey novel. Over the next three months, I wrote and completed my first novel of my author career called The Penalty.

Acknowledgements

I wouldn't be where I am today without my amazing parents, Fred and Michelle. There's a total of six of us under our roof, but yet I can't wrap around the thought of how much they work to keep up with all of us. We went through a lot in our lives, starting with my shingles virus and almost going blind in my left eye, then we fought through the 2007 financial crisis. Through all of that chaos, my parents have never stopped loving and caring for us. They support us anyway they can. I wouldn't have attended Full Sail University down in Florida if it wasn't for them. They've helped me reach my dream, and now I'm finally living it.

I have two older brothers (specifically half-brothers), Kain and Conner, and a younger sister, Mariah. Even though they can be annoying from time to time, I love them all. They have been riding along the same boat as me this whole time, and they've always been pushing me to do my best. I'm happy to have them in my life. They definitely keep me rolling on the tracks!

I don't even know how to start this next one, but I hope you go out in the world and find your second mom! Brittany, also known as Frau, my high school German teacher, is the real explosion of my author career lifting off. In high school, I didn't have a lot of teachers supporting me, but Frau held my hand and brought me on a journey of a lifetime! During my younger years in high school, I was actually addicted to film and wanted to make movies (which I'm still wanting to do). So, she would constantly find me film competitions whether they dealt with German in some shape or form, or just any local competitions. I ended up winning four film awards, three of them being German film contests! I remember when she helped me annoy the citizens of my hometown about the video that needed the most views to win. Frau presented my films in class, even my forty-minute travel vlog. She's been such a mother to me, and she still supports me to this day. I can never find a way to thank her enough, but she's definitely a bright star in my life's constellation.

After high school, with help from my parents, I flew down to Florida and had to rent out an apartment for college. During this time, I was actually reaching for my film degree. So, my school holds these special events that we can attend to learn about the entertainment industry. I've been going to quite a bit of the writing ones, but there was one that just blew my mind away, and it was hosted by two amazing Creative Writing professors. This is where I met my third mom, Carol. Carol gave an amazing presentation at the event, and when it was over, about thirty of us kids rushed over to her and began asking questions. I stayed in the back and just listened to her captivating stories while tears flushed out from her eyes. But one by one, the kids started to leave after they had their questions answered, and I remember two of us remained. The feeling I had was like no other. I didn't have a question for her or a need to say anything to her, but I was just stuck in mud. I felt like I just needed to keep listening to her; she was just amazing. She ends up inviting me to her writing workshop class where I would end up attending every month. She's taught me so much about screenwriting and storytelling, and she's swung my emotions all over the room that I ended up switching my film degree to Creative Writing. Without her in my life, this novel may have never of been written.

I ended up meeting two amazing friends in Carol's class, and they are Lindsay and Cambria. Lindsay is Carol's non-official student helper. She's so dedicated in movies and stories that she has a ginormous google drive with basically every screenplay in the world. She has pushed me so much and has taught me a lot while writing my novel. I actually met Cambria first. Cambria was mentoring in one my earlier entertainment classes, and when I snuck into Carol's class for the first time, guess who was sitting in the back row with her mouth dropped to the floor. Yep, it was Cambria. She was confused as to why I was there, but this is when we truly became friends. She's given me so much advice and was watching out for me in the sketchy state of Florida. Both Lindsay and Cambria spoiled me, and they still spoil me to this day. I wish we lived close to one another, but we'll plan meetups in the future.

I also want to shout out my Creative Writing Director at school, Wes. I'd always ask a question on choices I need to make or about writing in general, and no matter how giant my questions can get, he's there to support me all the way. He answers so fast, and he's kind enough to help me and other students in his free time.

My friends at home have been putting up with me since day one, and I can't wait to see what they accomplish in their futures. Ann-Marie has been my best friend since Kindergarten. We grew up with the exact same teachers through elementary school. Ever since kindergarten, Ann-Marie has had her hand on my shoulder. I remember the time when we went on our school Germany trip in high school, and both of us were drained out with all the drama, and we ended up venturing out into the wilderness, trespassing over some weird closure tape, and finding a waterfall. This had to be the best part about the trip because we were stranded from the drama and we were together in peace. Me and Ann-Marie have so many special moments in our lives that we've spent together. When I told her about my dream of becoming a writer, she's been cheering me on and supporting me through my journey.

I can't thank my friends enough. All of my friends including Zach, Alex, Trina, and Carson wished me luck to my success. They've kept in touch with my writing and helped me strive for success. They all fight through challenges and tough courses in their lives, and I'm just so lucky that they've kept me strolling on my feet. I have a few more friends that I want to give notice to. I met Liam, Barrett, Abby A., Kaitlyn, Abby B., and Amber Lowe through social media. I've probably annoyed them so much with my passion, but to this day, they keep telling me how excited they are to see me succeed in life. Some of them were even my critiquers for this novel! I thank you all for your support! I wish I could just see some of you in person.

My life wouldn't be the same without the people who sit beside me. Make your life the best life ever. We will end up looking back at it all like a movie. Make it one epic premiere!

About the Author

Ethan Marek is nineteen years old and resides with his family in New Prague, Minnesota. He's currently aiming for his BFA in Creative Writing at Full Sail University (2020). He teaches teenagers and young adults about his life struggles and how he fought through them with his stories. He loves to write weird and unique fiction stories that directs his readers to strange roads. He's a unique character himself as he has a tremendous love for hockey, and he's a selective eater who has anxiety when trying new foods. His all-time favorite snack is movie theater popcorn, and his favorite season is the snowy wintertime, right when hockey flares up.

Ethan's dream was originally a movie writer, but after experiencing the life in Florida at Full Sail University, he realized he would be too homesick living out in Hollywood. So, he took another direction to reach his dreams and made his movie ideas into novels. Some of his books may be in present tense because of his tremendous skill in screenwriting, but he can also choose to use past tense; it's just a creator's choice in the end.

Made in the USA
Middletown, DE
21 October 2021